Praise for Darin Bradley's *Totem*

"Incisive, scathing, and smart as hell, Darin Bradley's *Totem*, like his previous novel *Chimpanzee*, confronts us with the best and rarest kind of dystopia: that which only gently distorts and extrapolates from our own lived reality, leaving us with a world whose sociopolitical horrors are uncomfortably easy to recognize."

—Nicole Kornher-Stace, author of *Archivist Wasp*

"*Totem* is a brilliant, beautiful, challenging, scary novel. It's everything speculative fiction should be. I cannot recommend it enough."

—Jonathan Wood, author of *Anti-Hero*

"In this poetic, intimate, and visionary tale, Darin Bradley deftly explores what happens when international aid, crowd-funding, and online voyeurism gangs up, in a near future that seems almost too close for comfort."

—Berit Ellingsen, author of *Not Dark Yet*

Praise for Darin Bradley's *Chimpanzee*

"As with the best dystopian fiction, Chimpanzee taps into many contemporary issues and fears — in this case, everything from the surveillance state to the student-debt crisis. *Chimpanzee* is a post-collapse novel for those who have become numb to them, and a unique take on a subgenre in sore need of one. The book's dazzling originality not only helps overcome much of its dryness, it makes it well worth the extra homework."

—Jason Heller, NPR Books

"[A] disturbingly believable near-future dystopia."
—*Publishers Weekly*

"Excellent literary dystopia."
—Starred review, *Library Journal*

Praise for Darin Bradley's *Noise*

"An exceptionally polished debut."

–Publishers Weekly

"Considering the nature of his dystopic fiction and the fullness of his vision, I can perhaps be forgiven for thinking that, in his debut, Darin Bradley may be The One."

–Lincoln Cho, *January Magazine*

"A cruel little knife-strike of a book, in the best possible way."

–Jeff VanderMeer,
author of the *Southern Reach* trilogy.

"Edgy and disturbing, *Noise* is a worthy successor to all those post-holocaust books of yesteryear."

–Analog Magazine

"This is a stunner of a novel, with a modernist almost poetical style, and a concept that blasts its way through the hoary old clichés . . . It's the best fiction book I've read this year."

–Mark Rose, *Bookgasm*

"Darin Bradley's brainy, slippery, and riveting *Noise* is *Lord of the Flies* on serious psychotropics. With narrative tendrils in the 'paper' book and online as well, *Noise* is deliberately speaking to a young, media-soaked audience through various texts and tricks. You watch. *Noise* is destined to be a milestone work for Millennial readers."

–Barth Anderson,
author of *The Patron Saint of Plagues*
and *The Magician and the Fool*

Light Both Foreign and Domestic

Darin Bradley

Underland Press

Light

Both

Foreign
and
Domestic

Table of Contents

Light
Both
Foreign
and
Domestic

AROLD THINKS IT LOOKS LIKE A SPACE SHIP. OR SOMETHING. It makes him feel weird to look at it. Like, wrong somehow. The front seats face backward, their backs clean up against the dash where the steering wheel and the glove box should be. The back seats look normal enough, facing the way back seats do—only, were they still back seats now or just seats? There are sensors and things cupped against the edges of the windshields, and there is a round version of the flag painted on the hood identifying the Department of Transportation and some other federal sub-committee-or-other. It looks almost like a military insignia. Maybe a patch he'd have worn on his uniform, back when.

He stares at the car parked in his driveway. In Jolene's spot. Just . . . sitting there. People look at it as they drive by. As if he's in favor of this overreaching, nanny state bullshit. Just letting one of them on into the driveway, right there onto his property. Jim Webb told him something about this, Harold thinks. Who can remember? Cars without drivers? Harold can't believe it. The things are already broken—parking in people's driveways without permission. How is he supposed to edge the grass on that side with the thing parked so close to the lawn? It's Sunday, after all.

He walks around it until he finds all of the registrations and the FCC codes and whatnot stenciled on the trunk. He finds a number to call for assistance, and he ignores his neighbors.

"That is just ridiculous," Harold says. "I need to talk to your supervisor."

"I assure you, sir," the kid on the phone says, "he'll tell you the same thing."

"You can't just park these things on private property."

"We don't park them, sir. There are algorithms in the network that determine the best places to park based on public need."

"Well, whoever wrote that program should be fired."

"Sir, if you'll just wait, it'll leave as soon as someone in your town requests a ride."

"How long will that take?"

"Not long."

"If it's not gone in an hour, I'm towing it into the street."

"Sir, it's against the law to interfere with the cars' automation. That can endanger the network and other riders."

"It's *parked*. What harm can it do?"

"It's the law, sir."

"Goddammit."

Harold ends the call, and he stands at his living room window, staring through the blinds at the alien thing. He can hear a lawnmower running down the street. He goes to the hall closet and gets out his American flag and takes it out to the front porch. He unrolls it carefully on its pole and sets it into the mount on the porch rail. A kid watches him out in the street, shielding his eyes from the sun with his hand. It almost looks like he's saluting.

A radio from another world, Harold thinks. A dimension next door. He wonders if it could work that way. Jim Webb told him about this kind of thing, too. He tells Harold about all kinds of things. Harold doesn't listen to most of it. A man goes to the VFW for the company of quietude in all those bottles, among people who just want to share the silence. A man like Harold does, anyway. He doesn't go to remember better days—he goes not to remember these ones now. He remembers just fine being married and working a job and believing in some reason to bother with it all anyway. A better life gone by.

And now this. He needs some answers.

It was something about scientists, Jim Webb told him. They shoot light or something at sheets of metal and some of it slips through onto this collector, but some of it that lands there came from the past or the future. Or something. That's the only way they can explain it. Tiny time travelers made of light, getting sucked out of somewhere and jammed into a place where they don't want to be.

Harold knows something about that. He and Jolene were engaged before the draft. He didn't want to go anywhere, and she waited for him. He remembers what she looked like in a blue gingham dress with her hair done back. Waiting with all the others at the bus stop. That good day, despite the hippies and their signs. Finally back. He could feel her heart beating against his, straight through his uniform. That's how hard he squeezed her. She took a bunch of dancing lessons, while he was gone. It's the first thing he remembers her telling him.

Maybe the scientists' thing could work with radios, too, slipping signals in from somewhere else. Like the light, or something, which would explain what he's hearing. Pasts and presents that exist in their own right, different from whatever's actually going on.

This broadcaster, in the radio studio in Dallas, is talking about the National Weather Service and the new normal, and how they can expect unseasonal storm systems in July and August, even tornadic ones. Which is horseshit. That's too late for tornadoes in Texas.

Harold sees nothing but oceanic blue sky over the tops of the elms and post oaks lining Shadowbrook Street as he threads the truck between street-parked cars until he pulls onto Division and opens things up with a little gas. It's a busy Saturday at the Pack 'n Save when he drives past, and there isn't a cloud in the sky. Maybe they'll get weird rain in Dallas, but it looks just like summer here in Siwash. Maybe there's a tomorrow-world colliding with their own. A Dallas next door, where all the constant climate change and all that really is too far gone. Maybe he could get to some other future or past like that himself. Just drive on through with all his protons and all that. Someplace better, where those scientists are stealing all the light from a place where Jolene still is.

The caliche lot at the VFW shines like phosphorus in the sun. It crunches underfoot as Harold moves between the cars left there last night, as people caught rides or hooked up or just walked home. Like shoes in a living room—just a place to leave things. The digital sign for the First Siwash Bank, across the street, says it's 104 out. Harold believes it. There's no hope for a Texas summer.

It's a clean, bright day out. The kind that shows you things, whether you want them to or not. Jolene used to take him out in them all the time, and they had to see a counselor together before she learned that big groups of people can make him see things he'd rather not. A past he didn't have a say in, and there's all kinds of things that can resurrect the dead, even on the best days. Jolene learned it. She learned to drink with him to keep it all put. He didn't mind all the dancing. She liked it, and there isn't a bad time in a honky tonk. Never was.

Inside the VFW hall, it is immediately cool and dark. A place of survival under these concerns. He moves past the plaques and frames and lists of memorable people in the post. Kevin's got the TV on in the canteen, and nothing's playing on the stereo. There's nobody else drinking yet.

Kevin pulls a pint glass off his shelf and gets it under the Miller tap for Harold. Kevin takes the beer, and he makes a sound like he's deflating as he sits. An old man's sound.

Harold looks at the TV. There's some government people giving a press conference about the driverless cars. On a Saturday, no less. That would explain why Kevin hasn't got anything on the stereo. House rules, even if the post commander isn't around. You got to shut up for government business.

"One of those damn cars parked itself in my driveway," Harold says.

Kevin doesn't look away from the TV. "Did you ask it to?"

"Of course I didn't ask it to! What kind of question is that?"

"Well, what's it doing there?" Kevin says.

"I don't know. Waiting to take somebody on a ride I guess. I just can't believe it. Don't we already have Uber in town? Doesn't June's boy do that?"

"Barb's son," Kevin says. "Michael."

"You don't even pay for these rides. It's a tax dollars thing. Can you believe that?"

"I can believe it."

"Un-American is what it is."

Kevin doesn't say anything. He watches the press conference, and Harold watches it with him for a minute. He looks around at things as if he can't help it, and Kevin still has that picture of Harold from that New Year's tucked into the frame of the VFW motto on the wall, between the top shelves. *Honoring the dead by serving the living.* Harold backed his truck into the drainage ditch that night, trying to edge around all the cars in the packed lot, and it stayed there, despite a bunch of bother, and everybody made him come back into the bar, and they wrapped him in caution tape and took his red-faced picture and gave him more to drink. Hank Boedecker towed the truck out on New Year's Day after there was room to get around all the cars.

"Kevin," Harold says, "you seen Jim Webb lately?"

"Last week or so."

"I need to ask him about something he told me."

"All right."

He gets started on his second beer.

"POW flag's still crooked," Harold says.

"I know."

—⁓—

Hank Boedecker leaves the wrecker running in the street directly in front of Harold's driveway. The 4 is missing from Hank's phone number on the passenger door. The other numbers, curling at their faded edges, aren't long behind it. Harold guesses that this side of Hank's truck doesn't generate much business.

Hank pulls his ball cap down over his brow, then rights it again as he walks up.

"Hey, Harold."

"Hank."

Some of Harold's neighbors are out on their porches, hands on hips or shielding their eyes. It seems to Harold that, increasingly, that's the only way to look in his direction—by protecting your eyes. As if he is made of sun.

Hank gestures at the driverless car. "You going to follow me in that or something?"

"What?" Harold says. "I can't drive that."

Hank squints at Harold, and Harold wonders if Hank sees it too—that difficulty in regarding him."

"Drives itself, Harold," Hank says.

"Why would I want it to take me anyplace?" Harold says.

Hank chews on his bottom lip. The sound of his wrecker is steady behind them.

"Well," Hank says, "what did you call it here for?"

"That ain't it, Hank. I want you to tow it out my driveway."

"Why's it in your driveway?"

"I don't know. The government put it here."

There are more neighbors in their yards around them, having a look. Harold likes that they can see him doing something about all this.

"The gov— . . . The hell'd you do, Harold?"

"Nothing."

"Nobody's called it for a ride or nothing?"

"Not in twenty-four hours."

Hank looks at Harold's truck beside the car. "So you don't need me to tow your truck anyplace?"

"Truck's fine."

Hanks looks at the car. "Ugly, sonuvabitch, isn't it?"

"Yessir."

Hank tries to open the door.

"It's locked."

"I know."

"We got to get it out of gear, or it's going to mark up your driveway."

"I don't care."

"All right then, let me get the truck lined up."

⁂

The police cruiser chirps its siren when it pulls up. It's Jeff Arnold. Harold helped him plumb his French drains, back when all that water kept pooling in Jeff's back yard during the tornado season. The *real* tornado season.

He takes his time getting out of the car, and Hank and Harold just stand quietly, staring at him until he makes his way over.

"What are y'all doing?" Jeff says.

Hank looks at Harold. "This thing's stuck in Harold's driveway."

Jeff looks at it. He smiles at Harold. "Probably the best place in town for it, don't you think?"

Hank laughs, but Harold just looks at Jeff. "Very funny. I want this thing off my property."

Jeff studies it. "Why'd it pick your place?"

"I don't know. Some algorithm."

"Some what?" Hank says.

"Never mind."

Jeff surveys all the neighbors. "Well, y'all best quit messing with it. You can't tow it. It's against the law."

Harold gives Jeff a good look. "Did somebody call you out here, Jeff?"

The dispatcher squawks in the receiver on Jeff's shoulder. He listens to the codes, then looks at Harold. "Just leave it alone. Call and tell them it's broken."

"I did."

"Call again, but leave it alone."

He walks back to his cruiser. The dispatcher has more to say as he goes.

They watch him go, and they stand in the sound of the wrecker.

"Sorry, Harold," Hank says. "Maybe call it like you want a ride. Just leave it stranded someplace."

⸺

Harold follows the prompts on his phone and downloads the app for the cars. It verifies his information with its database, and Harold adjusts his reading glasses and taps the request for a car. The app tells him it is retrieving data and preparing his ride. He makes sure to choose the icon of the car that looks like the one in his driveway.

The house is clean around him. The housekeeper must have come by yesterday. His coffee steams in little, respiring clouds, and the TV is quiet in the living room. He muted it in case he had to talk to anybody to do this.

The app tells him his car will be ready in twenty minutes.

He gets up and goes outside and waits for it to unlock its doors. He waits beside it for a long time, and he watches the app, waiting for the car to power up or do what it's going to do. Out of sleep mode or whatever it's doing. He wonders what he is going to do with that part of his driveway, after it's gone, now that the area is precious to him. He liked it empty because it had a function for Jolene's car, until it didn't, and he doesn't think it's right to change that.

After the timer runs out, another car, like the one in his driveway, rolls quietly up to the spot where Hank parked his wrecker. A blinking light on the door frame tells him that he can get inside. His app shows him that it has arrived, and it shows him that it drove over from Minnie Falls.

He looks at the car in Jolene's spot, but it is inert. The two cars don't say anything to each other. No bleeps or flashes or TV robot noises. There are simply two, when there should be one. An extra photon, in from next door—a world nearby.

Harold dismisses the new car, and it rolls silently away. He deletes the app from his phone, and his coffee isn't very warm anymore in its mug.

———

Harold watches the rain while he waits. It's a heavy rain, a concerted rain, as if the drops, collectively, are making a real go at something. He thinks about how far each fell, through winds and thermals, all the way to exactly where each one lands, making tiny dry spots somehow significant. The force of it is knocking leaves out of his black walnut tree onto the truck and the car. There are branches fallen in a few yards. The petrichor is strong enough that he can smell it through the windows, even though they're closed.

He thinks of other times in his life, watching other bombardments of rain on other leaves, pulling apart branches with the shells and claymore mines pulling apart his friends. The jungle floor will make mud of any man, and those that get out of it are just automations of themselves anyway. Animated by mud and carrying out the tasks of being themselves as ordered for the rest of their useful lives, despite the best efforts of shrinks and support groups and gentle spouses with their fingers on your forehead, forced to take part in relived conversations and battlefield confessions when those they've married slip into a past they don't want to attend. The only thing for it is the company of others, who've been there, at a bar so you can drink enough to sleep at night.

The hold music stops on his phone.

"Thank you for waiting," a woman says. "How can I help you?"

Harold pulls his mind back out of the rain. How long has he been holding a cup of coffee? He swallows to get his throat working.

"Yes," he says. He isn't even angry. "I'm calling about the car in Siwash. Siwash, Texas."

"Yes, sir. Did you have a bad experience during your ride?"

"No, you see, it's broken. I think."

"Broken? How, sir?"

"It doesn't move. It hasn't moved in days. It's just been in my driveway."

"Really? One moment."

Harold listens to the sounds of keyboards and conversations on the other end of the line. It takes a village, he supposes.

"I'm sorry, sir. The transponder for that unit reports several operations over the last seventy-two hours, at all times of day."

"That's impossible," Harold says. "I'm looking at it right now. It hasn't moved."

He hears more typing.

"Please," he says, "I don't mean to be a problem again. Could you just send someone to reboot it or something? Get it doing what it's supposed to be doing?"

"You haven't been a problem, sir," she says. "But yes, of course. I'll put in a work order, and we'll get someone out this evening."

"Thank you."

The rain hasn't let up, and it's relentless against Harold's windshield, as if it has urgent business and it won't take no—or a piece of tempered glass—for an answer. His windshield wipers hammer at it, and he can't really get the radio loud enough over its roar to hear it, so he just turns it off and listens to the truck at work. The pools that his wheels kick up against the undercarriage—sudden, short sizzling sounds, like cauterized wounds. The protests of the wipers' motors with each beat and the punch of them hitting their terminal sweeps and jerking back for another go. It feels like his heartbeat, as if he is inside himself—a hot, tight core deep within the body's critical functions while his outer self takes the rain's pounding. A hidden trauma identity. A sun—what it's really like in there, under the unbearable surface where the laws of chemistry and physics and time travel and all that write themselves.

The lot outside the VFW looks alive as water trembles in its divots. There are a few other cars around, despite the storm, and Harold gets out under his semi-functional umbrella and makes it inside with only wet shoulders and legs. He thinks about all the effort that goes into keeping the face dry, specifically, even after all that time in rains where it didn't matter and you had no choice and an umbrella would've just been sniper bait.

Kevin has George Jones on the stereo. The TVs are silent as they rotate through super-Doppler reports and county maps warning who to expect what when. Calling a future that doesn't exist yet, reporting the things to come as if the weathermen can make it true with just the saying of it. Harold is pretty wet, and there is already water on the floor in the canteen where the others dripped it, so he leaves his umbrella in the corner under the coat rack and takes a stool next to Jim Webb at the bar. Kevin gets a pint glass under the Miller tap for him.

"POW flag's still crooked, Kevin," Harold says.

"I know it," Kevin says. He puts the beer in front of Harold.

Jim's got half a longneck bottle of Bud in front of him, and he looks happy about it. Harold can't tell how long Jim's been here, but he can bet that's his first beer, however long it's been. He doesn't drink them fast, or in quantity.

Jim was Air Force. Harold thinks he probably didn't get too rained on. He was an inside guy. Maps, Harold thinks he remembers. Drawing terrain and transportation like chessmen. Fixing the world in place in joint operations that always left Harold feeling as is there wasn't a certain place in the entire goddamn country.

"Hank told me about that car in your driveway," Jim says. "Strangest thing."

Harold feels like it just joined them in the room. A third wheel in a private conversation. Or waiting for him out in the lot, rolling up quiet, the way they do. There's a crack of thunder, and he hopes some lightning fries its electronics, wherever it is.

"Strange, all right," Harold says, "but I took care of it today."

He gestures at Kevin for another beer. He drinks to mean it.

"Really?" Jim says.

"Thing's broke," Harold says. "I called them and said so. They think it keeps going places, but it doesn't. When they get into its logs or whatever, they'll see. They'll need to get it back to its shop or someplace."

Harold drinks his beer. It isn't very good, and he doesn't really like it, but it's the cheapest thing Kevin keeps on tap. He could actually afford better drinks now. There aren't any medical bills left to pay, and the grocery bill is a lot lower. Car insurance, too. Has been for a while, he supposes, but he's used to the Miller, and Kevin pours it for him without asking. Harold likes that. He gets different drinks on New Year's or if someone has a reception in the canteen. Special occasions. He drinks Miller on those nights, too. He just also drinks other drinks.

"Listen, Jim," Harold says. "I been meaning to ask you about something you said."

Jim drinks a little of his beer. "What'd I say?"

"A while back," Harold says. "About nearby dimensions and light particles from the future and all that."

Jim's face brightens. "Well, what about it?"

"How far's it go?" Harold says.

"What do you mean?"

"I mean," Harold says, "is it only light? I mean what else gets through sometimes? To our universe."

"I think it's everything," Jim says.

"Everything's getting through?" Harold says. That would explain this weird damn weather and those cars and Jolene and everything else. All of it into his life from the wrong place and time.

Jim thinks. He flags Kevin down for another beer. Harold checks, but Jim's first bottle isn't even empty. Harold likes this.

He gives Kevin a nod too when he comes over, and he finishes the last half of his pint in a hurry to make space for a fresh one. Him and Jim, drinking together. He likes it.

"Well, see," Jim says, "I don't know all about it, but I've read some on the internet."

"That's all right, Jim. Go on."

"Light's the only thing we know, I think—that they can measure, anyway. The way between things seems to be light."

Harold takes the beer when Kevin sets it down. He doesn't notice himself doing it.

"But that doesn't mean it's all," Jim says. "Way some of them think, every time you make a decision or take a right turn or anything, there's a different universe that branches off where you did something different. Made the other choice. Just like all those quantum states appearing in superposition in the photon experiment."

Harold thinks about it. He ignores the part that doesn't mean anything to him. "Every decision? That's a lot of damn universes."

Jim smiles. "Yeah there's a lot of math involved."

"So the best outcome happens to you, all the time, in some better version of the universe?" Harold says.

"I hadn't thought about it like that."

"When you get the shit results, the shit universe, you're giving yourself in a new branching-off universe or whatever a better go of it. Everybody is. All the time."

"I suppose so."

Harold looks at the VFW motto in the frame on the wall behind the bar. *Honoring the dead by serving the living.*

"You think maybe there's a place where me and Jolene are just fine. Like, there's that for them on account of me living this worse option here?"

Jim looks at him for a long time.

"There might be, Harold."

Harold nods. He asks Kevin for two shots of whiskey.

Harold hands over his keys when Kevin demands them. Harold knows better than to fight him on this. Letting somebody out of the bar a little loose is one thing—if you can't tell too much. Letting a regular like Harold out when he's still trying to count empty shot glasses on the bar is entirely something else. Harold wouldn't let Kevin take them while they were drinking. Like collecting trophies. They did this together. Earning campaign ribbons.

"We'll get your truck home tomorrow," Kevin says.

Harold thinks the rain might've let up. He can't tell. How long have they been in here?

"Settle up your tab when you can do math," Kevin says.

"You're cutting me off, Kevin?"

"I'm cutting you off."

Harold points at the keys. "But I'm not driving."

"I'll get him home," Jim says. Harold doesn't think Jim looks very drunk, but they've both been at it. Putting them back. Trading stories about the things wives do.

"You all right?" Kevin says to Jim.

"Yeah. Probably pushing it, but we'll be all right."

"All right, then. Y'all don't want to call Michael and get his Uber?"

"Nah. He don't need to be out in this weather. Barb would kill us."

Harold stares at the weather report on the TV. They haven't let up all evening. He's not sure what they're trying to tell him anymore.

"Come on, Harold."

He follows Jim into the rain. Did he bring an umbrella? They move across the lot at a clip, and Jim gets his sedan open and they fall into it like it's some kind of evac. Harold sits there while Jim goes through all the pre-flight knobs and keys to get them going. Did John Alvarez come by earlier? Shit. He isn't sure.

"Thanks, Jim," Harold says. He surprises himself with the saying of it.

"Oh, you're not too far out of the way," Jim says. "You'd do the same for me."

"I meant the drinks."

The windshield wipers pound the silence between them.

"I know it's been hard, Harold."

"Yeah."

"You can call me anytime, you know. You don't have to sit alone if you don't want to."

Harold tries to figure that out, and it seems complicated.

"One more thing," Harold says. "the universe—universes—once you branch off to a new one, there ain't no going back? Not like the lights that bring the past and the future together."

Jim drives carefully. He's keeping it slow.

"I don't suppose so."

"You can't go back the way those lights do. Universe to universe." Harold tries to gesture what he means with his hands.

"Well," Jim says, "I suppose if they were entangled, like the photons. You can't separate them across any distance—or time, apparently. Maybe even dimensions."

"What?" Harold says.

"Entangled. I had to look it up," Jim says. "Pretty bizarre. It's part of that experiment."

"Time knows no bounds, huh?"

"Something."

"What do they entangle?"

"Just light, I think."

"But maybe other things, too?"

"Yeah, maybe."

Jim turns them onto Shadowbrook, and there are limbs down in the yards from the storm.

"Look at that," Harold says. "Safe and sound. I guess we're the good universe this time, huh?"

Jim laughs. "I guess so."

He pulls up in front of Harold's house, and there is the driverless car in Jolene's old spot. Harold looks at it for a long time.

"Well. Thanks, Jim."

He gets out into the rain.

—⸗—

Harold isn't sure if he got down on the floor because the storm sirens are blowing or because he just got down on the floor. How long has he been down here? He can hear the siren closest to him, in the elementary school soccer fields, on Pearl Street. He can hear it moaning, louder than anything in the room. The wind's as loud as a Huey's rotors, and it's really giving it to the house. He gets to his knees, but he doesn't stand all the way up straight. You don't do that when you're moving through rotorwash. Might get a head chopped off or something if you get in the habit and end up under a tiny Sioux heli one day without thinking about it.

He's got to get Jolene out back into the storm shelter. It takes her longer to get down the metal ladder, since they scoped her kneecap last month. It's taking a while to heal. Why did he mute the TV? A tornado warning is in effect. He should take shelter immediately. In the event of a real attack, they may only have minutes to get into the shelter before the bombs hit and turn Shadowbrook Street into an incandescent otherworld. A place it shouldn't be under anything but the worst human circumstances. Siwash is too close to all the aircraft manufacturers in Dallas and Fort Worth. They're on Russia's target list for sure. He'd have to report in as soon as he got Jolene safe. She'd sing to comfort herself while he was gone. She did that all the time, whenever she didn't like something. Usually straight through tornado warnings, and he liked the sound of it down there off the concrete walls in the shelter. She always kept hold of the ladder with one delicate hand, as if to keep herself put.

"Jolene! Get out of bed!"

The bottle in his hand lifts itself to his mouth, and he takes another drink. She won't like that he's drunk. He tries not to get that way around her. Except on New Year's or special occasions.

The storm siren keeps spinning up on its pole, like an electric banshee that can't make up her damn ear-splitting mind which way she wants to shout. Making sure everyone hears her.

He'll give Jolene a second. Now that it's got into her spine, she doesn't move so fast. She won't want his help out of bed. It pisses her off.

"Hurry up!"

He opens the front door, and the wind is a huffing engine now. Sonuvabitch must be close by. There are tree limbs down everywhere. On cars and things and piles of hail. He can see other people on their porches, waiting for the thing, to behold it. A funnel of God with the wrath to prove it.

He sees the driverless car in his driveway, covered in fresh green leaves torn from his black walnut tree. Where the hell is his truck? He remembers. It's at the canteen, taking a better universe without him, still and whole in that parking lot, where he can't mess it up.

He stares at Jolene's spot, and he has another drink because she's not here to get mad about it. Dammit—he left his American flag in its post, out in this weather. It's a breach of flag protocol. He puts the bottle down and pulls the pole out of the mount. He has to get down in the bushes, out from under the porch to do it. And the rain hits him sideways, and the flying branch ripped from his or somebody else's tree clubs him in the temple. He knows to blink very rapidly because that's how you get your sight back when some bastard flash-bangs you. He stands there with his hands on his head long enough to wonder how long he's been doing it, then his hands come away slick with his blood in the lightning, and the rain washes them off, and he puts them back on the wound and checks again. He's bleeding pretty good, even if this tornado keeps washing it away.

It's hard walking in all that wind to the car, but he probably needs to get to a hospital. He tries the door handles, and they're locked. He bangs his fist on the windows, but they don't crack. Doing it makes him woozy. He stops, and he just rests his palm on the car, right up on the roof, and they don't do anything, either one of them, riding out a new shitty universe. Doing himself a favor in a universe nearby where he probably didn't have so much to drink and is sitting in his shelter, following the radio and resting his feet in the lawn chair that was Jolene's.

Harold wonders how it works. What's the shift like, stepping into new universes every passing instant, leaving himself—and others—behind. Are there flashes of light or something when it happens, and he just doesn't see them? Or if somebody's *entangled* with something, if that's really a thing, and keeps ripping it out of different dimensions and dropping it where they think it belongs, whether they realize it or not. He needs to look it up. Is that what God means by "a plan?" He has one for everybody, but what if that's just one *version* of everybody. Things go the way He intends all the time, just people don't see it. Somewhere, one of Harold already knows these answers, siting up there with Him, bugging Him with questions about how it all worked down here.

His phone rings, and he passes the front door to get it. He can see through the window where the whiskey bottle is sitting upon the porch. It didn't even fall over. His flag is in the bushes, twisted up.

"Hello?"

"Mr. Harold?"

"Hi, Alice." He looks around. The place could use her touch again. Is she supposed to come today? She probably has stuff to clean around her own place, after the storm. "Y'all okay?"

"Yes, we are fine."

"Well, good. Hell of a storm!" He touches his temple. It stopped bleeding at some point, but he could still use a stitch or two.

"Mr. Harold, I am not coming anymore."

"What? You mean today?"

"No, anymore."

"Well, why not, Alice?"

"Yesterday, I came, and there were government men in your driveway."

"You came during all that rain? What were they doing?"

"They were working on your new car."

"It's not my— What did they do?"

"They worked under its hood until they closed it, and it went away."

"It went away?"

"I'm sorry, Mr. Harold. I don't want to be around government men."

He doesn't say anything for a moment. How can he blame her? She needs to make a better world for herself, too.

"It's okay, Alice. I understand."

"Goodbye, Mr. Harold."

Harold guesses it sounds like a phone call, when universes change.

There are mowers and chippers out in all the lawns, creating a mechanized drone as everybody drags things into piles or chops them up. There's his truck, back in his spot, inert. The keys are in the ignition, and it sits there waiting on him to decide how things go now, every passing instant. Harold feels paralyzed by it. He thinks about the messed-up weather and global warming and all those trucks and cars everywhere, just burning up gas and making things worse. It's a group effort, ruining this planet to save it for versions of themselves somewhere else. He likes being a part of that. He's not alone in the endeavor.

He unspools the water hose from the caddy up against the wall and gets the water going. It takes him a few minutes, but he goes after his truck with the spray nozzle. He gets all the leaves sprayed off it, and when he's done, it drips in the rising light, clean as he can get it. He puts the hose back and turns off the water, and the driverless car is still covered in debris. He looks at the two vehicles, and he goes back to the hose, and he washes the damn car off, and his neighbors drive by, watching, and they see his flag in the bushes.

There's eggs been thrown at it, the next morning. But not his truck. He doesn't see the shells anywhere. Just unfertilized chicken goop in dried splats and runnels all over the back. Unrealized potential, he thinks. Just something to eat, or mess cars up with.

Harold goes to the canteen, but there's nobody there but Kevin. Harold lifts the beer to his mouth like he's breathing. A body at work, doing important things without even involving him.

"You still got that car in your driveway?" Kevin says.

"Yeah."

"I thought you said they fixed it." Kevin watches the TV while he talks. Harold doesn't recognize the music on the stereo.

"They did. It doesn't work that way."

Kevin nods. Harold wonders if he knows he's doing it.

"There's more of them in town now," Harold says. "I guess in every town. I see them, driving around."

"Maybe it ain't the same one, then. Parking in your driveway."

"It's the same one."

"Well," Kevin says, "there's jobs, making them things. You see more old people at the Pack 'n Save now. Getting around."

Harold lifts his beer, then he puts it back down. He decides to *decide* to drink it.

"Say," Harold says, "you ever think sometimes a bad decision is the right thing to do?"

"All the time."

"No, I mean, like, getting into a shit situation or something."

Kevin looks at him. "I don't think about stuff like that."

"Why not?"

"What's the point?"

"No kidding. Who's even in charge, huh?"

Kevin doesn't say anything for a minute. He watches the TV. "You hear John Alvarez has to get his gall bladder out?"

Harold takes a slow drink. He enjoys it.

"I suppose it's catching on," Harold says.

"What?"

"Never mind. Hey, you fixed the POW flag."

Kevin looks. "No. Not me."

Harold drinks his beer steadily, evenly, until it's empty. He sets the empty glass down. "What do I owe you, Kevin?"

"That's all tonight?"

"That's all for now. I think I'm going away. I need a change."

"All right, then. That's on the house."

"See you, Kevin."

"See you."

⌇

Harold stands behind the car in his driveway, and he reads the service phone number stenciled on the back of the trunk again and enters it into his phone. The streetlight in his neighbor's yard gives everything a nice, orange glow. The cicadas are rattling in the trees, and he can hear traffic, not far away, on Division Street.

He looks at that orange light on everything while he navigates his phone through the customer service menus. Everything looks hot and wet with that light on it, and he imagines light both foreign and domestic smashing into everything without a care for which universe it's doing it in.

"Good evening, my name is Marsha. How can I help you?"

Harold thinks Jolene would have been good at Marsha's job. She liked people. She was the best receptionist at the office, even without his bias.

"Hi, Marsha. I'm sorry. I just got out of my ride, and I left my reading glasses inside. The doors are locked, and I can't get in."

"I'm so sorry, sir. The computer may need to be reset. Can you read me the serial number off the back of the trunk?"

Harold reads her the number, and she asks him to wait just a moment, and then the thing wakes up, and there's a light on the doorframe telling him he can get in.

"The vehicle should be unlocked now, sir."

"Yes, ma'am, it sure is. Thank you very much."

Harold ends the call, and he puts his hand on the car's roof, just to feel it again, and he opens the door and gets inside. There are dials in the console between the seats, and he sits in a back one because he wants to face the right way. He can still hear the cicadas through the windows, but they sound very far away. There is an electronic sound to the car as it goes about lighting its panels and displays. The headlights come on when he buckles his seatbelt, and they paint his garage door the color of sunlight.

Harold taps the interface screen on the console, and it has a destination button, so he presses that. It asks him for his destination in clear, glowing letters. Harold presses the record button so it will listen, and it shifts to green so he knows it's paying attention.

"I want to be right here, but somewhere else."

He lets go of the record button, and it tells him it's thinking. He leans back and closes his eyes. He doesn't want to do anything. He wants to be swept along with everyone else's better decisions. He feels sorry for all the versions of himself he's screwing over, but there are always victims of somebody's better thinking, like all those men, dead in the jungle or on the beach, thanks to the military's best ideas. The dead he needs to honor, and the living he still has to help. He thinks about Jim Webb's big ideas and how you can need something so badly in enough universes that it starts not to matter which one it shows up in. If there aren't any aliens out there in space, on any other Earths—if they're as alone as it feels—then that means him and everybody else are the only ones anywhere thinking about it. The consciousness of the cosmos. The rules get weird in time and space. Anything is possible.

Harold opens his eyes, and there's light all over his garage door. He gets out of the car and stares at it, and after a minute, it powers down and locks its doors. He leaves it in Jolene's spot and gets in his truck and drives to the canteen. John Alvarez is at the bar, and he's pointing at his gut and explaining something to Kevin behind the bar, who just stares at him. When he notices Harold, he gets a glass under the Miller tap for him. There's a bunch of chatter over by the pool tables, and Jim Webb's got a paperback, and he's sitting at his own table. He looks up.

"Hey, Harold. Where you been?"

Hotels and Other Forms of Collapse

THIS IS NOT MY STORY—LET ME BE CLEAR. A MAN, WHO IS sometimes a woman, threw it at me.

Really, I think he was throwing it away, out his car window—a cigarette butt with its own syntax, a poetics suddenly beyond its burning. But there it was, exploding in smoldering, disappearing bits, being a story all over the sidewalk.

That, itself, is the story. All of it. It acquired me while I smoked a cigarette of my own, and then ended there.

When the smoker launched his cigarette, I recoiled. The butt came to rest at my heel, its expiring ember an uneven, carbonized mouth—the still-hot contour of a cauterized limb.

Unharmed, unbutted, I watched the Buick drive away. A curl of the man's vanishing smoke narrated itself into—

I watched the hipster recede in my rearview mirror. When he started walking slowly, pointedly, after me, I picked up Marxism and pulled it, a hoary and prickled sweater, over myself. I wasn't interested in this kid —how he'd come between Anna and me.

Soon enough, he disappeared into the gravity well of rearview perspective, bourgeois neon and streetlights lighting him away.

I realized too late that he had acquired this up there. This flash of story. I hadn't wanted to be in any paragraph. And because he hadn't known Anna was in

—this.

I tried to walk away, but it was the wrong direction. This is because I already know the driver: he studies art downtown with the soft-haired, Bohemian dream who, until an hour ago, slept with, loved with, and fucked with me. Regularly. When everything is connected by plot, causal is as causal does. This is all a story, as I've said, because it's his. A stranger's tale would've just been garbage.

I pulled a cigarette from my lapel pocket, lit it with my remaining match and started smoking my own story, now hopelessly pursuing the Buick-cum-Marxism (which is one of the faster philosophies).

He had to do something about the man's cigarette butt. No one ever noticed narrative litter, and they wouldn't until he started throwing it back.

He walked, after the Buick, toward her apartment, for under these circumstances, she waited in all directions.

I found him outside Seattle, easily enough when I lifted the entire Northwest and granny-tossed it over my head. It fell over me completely that way. Standing just to the side of Portland, I pulled this part of the smoker's story out of another pocket and wiggled into it with a sharp eye on "I found him outside Seattle, easily enough . . ." That did it.

This was a smoking coffee shop, which made me nervous. I once worried about vintage-wear, cover charges, and the demographics in lecture halls—now every ashtray was its own library, an entire history. This one the Bolshevik Revolution, that one photosynthesis. God only knew what He was doing in the coffee.

All of this was a much bigger problem than being attacked by a story with an axe to grind.

I concentrated on this line to bring things back into focus.

"Hey, . . . man," I said to the other guy—who had, really, never hit me with this. He made it up after all—I did say it was his story—or it made itself up. Either way.

I didn't want to just call him "man," so I balled "Joseph" in my fist and hit him with it. It splattered "Andrew" all over me in a thousand back-splashing bits. I'd explain, but the devil's in the details. Literally.

—

"Cute," Joseph said, smoking.

"What?"

"Mystery."

Joseph watched a girl in cat-glasses walk by, a slender, unending cigarette between her paintbrush fingertips. Andrew watched too, detached—her details seemed infinite, every instant further beyond his reach.

Joseph meant to put her in his pocket later. Have a conversation in a hotel over room service and bathrobes. I could tell he wanted me to make her willing—to like him and the idea. Otherwise he'd be in conflict with himself.

I felt bad for him: he hadn't wanted to be here in the first place—no one does. You can't write yourself into a story.

"Hold on," Andrew said, sitting. "You threw—or didn't throw" he looked confused "a cigarette at me, and it had, like, a story in it. This story."

You threw myself at myself, Andrew realized.

Joseph sighed. "I didn't do it on purpose. I didn't even really do it at all."

This place was clearly Joseph's territory. Others like him, like her, milled around them everywhere. Andrew was interloping, driven by his own suspicions about things that come too close.

He glared at Joseph. "Still"

"But the *mystery*," Joseph said, "nice. Now it's a story for certain, and you've dragged us both into it. Or it into us."

Joseph smiled at the girl with the glasses, thinking of girls who'd worn the same once before, only under different definitions of "cool" then, when he'd noticed such things studying design at Community. Some years prior.

It's nice of him, I think, to characterize himself. Only his ideas about Warhol and Seurat are stories unto themselves and have nothing to do with reality. Better that he leave himself to me.

—

"Yeah? Great," Andrew says now, stuffing his hands into his pockets. He's glaring nervously at a napkin on the floor. "So, what, we just toss meaningless pablum at each other for a while, and I eventually walk away knowing less about whatever than I did before?"

Joseph is uncertain if Andrew is still speaking to him. "Well, with words like 'pablum,' yeah," he says.

"I was better off on the sidewalk. In the beginning."

Joseph laughs—I've gone ahead and put the girl in his pocket. He doesn't realize what stories will unfold with her. What glasses of orange juice and domestic negotiations and nights of quiet boredom.

"You were never on the sidewalk," Joseph says. "And that wasn't the beginning."

———

Joseph left me there via a page from a Gideons Bible. When he'd finished his coffee, he stretched the page over himself like a giant condom. It wadded itself up and settled next to one of the table's splay-footed legs. When I flattened it back out, it was nothing but Holy Writ again.

I sat there, surrounded by smoke and chatter, my nerves, like fire, consuming themselves—and me along with them. A pair of muted TVs hung from ceiling poles in the back corners of the shop, and I watched them for a little while, afraid, really to do anything else. They showed commercials mostly.

I weighed options for a while, considering heaving geometry and hummingbirds and plates of fava beans at this mystery. I'd pick at the seams of postcolonialism, and slip between gaps in the disappearance at Roanoke to get some answers.

But really, what would I find?

And that's ultimately what I'd take from Joseph, only he'd be called Anna then, which is the name of the girl wearing the cat glasses who has accompanied him out via a thing I did with his pockets, her infinite lines streaming heartbreakingly behind.

I could throw whatever I wanted at the problem, yet here it would remain.

But there was the matter of Andrew, who was also stranded in this coffee shop. This wasn't his fault.

—⁓—

They had gone to Florida, between semesters. Andrew used the granny-toss again, uncertain how else to throw things at himself. Be-sandaled and be-shortsed now, he moved into the hotel, dodging valet parkers and bell hops.

He found Joseph and Anna on the twelfth floor. Joseph answered the door in his bathrobe, a tumbler of orange juice in his off-hand. He glanced at Anna before letting Andrew in.

Anna sat on the edge of one of the beds. She had folded her left leg up under herself, exposing it in a wedge through the gap in her robe. She smiled at Andrew as she tucked her cropped hair behind her ears.

"Hey," she said.

Joseph closed the door, squelching the hallway's yellowed, Saran light. It condensed itself into an eye, a tiny, outside dot winking through the peephole.

"Yeah, hey," Joseph said.

"She knows," Andrew hesitated, "about us?"

Anna tucked her other leg under herself. "What about you?"

Andrew stared, uncertain how to explain his and Joseph's bizarre relationship or the narrative invasion or how it had all already ended. He didn't want her to be an unwilling part of the problem.

Sunlight striped itself through the louvers on the window. They clacked against one another in the air-conditioned breeze. The stripes didn't quite reach Anna.

Joseph stepped past Andrew and into Anna. She was now holding Joseph's juice in her hand, blinking at Andrew behind her vintage eyeglasses.

"She knows now," she said.

It would be nice, Andrew realized, to sit with Anna. To watch re-runs on the hotel television, with the louvers thrown wildly open, exposing the insides of the room to the sunlight, exposing bathrobes and underwear to a world that it would be fun to pretend was watching—could watch—outside, below. They would take extra showers and try to look casual when they secured an evening cab to find some club, or perhaps a bar that would be more exciting, they would tell themselves, because it's here and not where they'd come from. And it would be. The story can come from anywhere.

Andrew would like to find out about Anna, about what he missed at the beginning. To have sex with her. Feeling better, he pulls Joseph back out of her and onto himself, leaving the couple alone again.

"This is better," Anna says, stretching upon the bed, revealing underwear that, despite the positioning of the louvers, the entire world can see.

Joseph lies down beside her. She's agreed to drive with him. They've rented a car that will become available tomorrow, when they will check out, their skins and fingernails scoured clean and dry by the hotel's so-hard water. They will have had sex quietly and will be excited about starting a new chapter.

Anna sets the juice down upon the fingerprint-ghosted varnish smoothing the nightstand. She rests the glass upon their paperwork, upon their agreement with the rental agency, which lists the make and model of the car they will drive out of Florida, back into the Northwest, and down neoned roadways. It even lists the people they will pass on the sidewalk.

Two

THE CLAMOR OF THE OTHER PATRONS CONSPIRED WITH MY nerves. In concert, they waged a stronger battle than I—sitting here seemed like an inactive retreat, like an unfair fight.

I snubbed out my cigarette and grabbed our empty glasses. "Sugar?"

I smirked—it was a joke between us, a sarcasm born some months earlier from a night of creamy ales and too-dark coffee.

Darcy smiled: "No."

On my way to the counter, I noticed several regulars with the hack—they stared at each other with dancing expressions, silent. The relay implant was nothing new—scensters had been sliding network cones into their necks for at least a year—but the hack had traded a retinal interface for the old semantic manifold. More importantly, it exploited ports. With a good connection, a few glances in the right sequence opened up the cortical node, and the neurons began to gibber. Emil promised me that a pair of these pre-cognitive geysers could fill a network channel with the slickest, darkest curves of perception. He likened it to wading through an abstract portrait. It went beyond this useless language.

The regulars looked a bit obscene, sitting there, swimming through each other's brains.

I couldn't wait to paint them.

When I returned, sloshing beer onto the table, Darcy examined the cigarette between her fingers. It bothers her when there's even the slightest imperfection, which there rarely is because she keeps her cigarettes in a little, chrome case.

She exhaled through the corner of her mouth. "So, did you get it?"

I reached for her lighter. "You know I didn't."

She punched a command into her relay before coiling it into her cigarette pack. She was the only one I knew who still packed her relay according to the manufacturer's suggestion. It took her forever to answer her calls like that.

She looked at me. "But Emil's still offering?"

I'd known Emil for a few years—he could still machine parts for combustion engines and knew how to fix transistors. Recently, he'd learned to execute the hack. He couldn't implant the hardware—too bloody, he said—but he had a cousin who could.

"I didn't get it," I said, cramming my cigarette between my lips. "He wanted to do it tonight. I said I had plans."

Darcy looked away. "I don't like the scars."

"You're not supposed to," I said, glancing at the divots puckering the hollows behind the other regulars' ears. "When the program goes normal, you'll pay out your ass for it. The scars are about free expression while it's still free."

I decided not to mention Emil's new MEMS, a legion of nanoscopic dermoplasts that wanted only vitamin E and a weekend to eat scar tissue. Once Emil got the rogue machine code out of the bots' little, remote foreman, he could retire—wealthy beyond imagination and minus one patent. I fought a laugh: watching the remote create viral relays out of every un-wired object in Emil's shop had resulted in a room full of beeping hijinks and a *very* expensive remodeling fee. The damn thing re-created itself *everywhere*, and Emil still hadn't figured out what it wanted—where it was trying to go.

Darcy peered over her glasses. "Look, this'll be easier if you don't—"

"I said didn't get it!"

I recoiled, and silence gathered between us.

I thought about

the spill of oncoming headlights—they silhouetted my hand atop the steering wheel. I glanced at Darcy: her glasses shone with the lurid glow of passing neon.

"I don't know," she said. "What do you think?"

My heart kept pace with the engine. "Maybe we're running this into the ground. Maybe it's time. For real."

In the pause that followed, Darcy turned down the radio—she always did when she wanted to speak. Sometimes when she wanted to listen. I ashed my cigarette into the wind.

"But, I don't know," I said. "Maybe we're just trying to talk ourselves into this."

Emil had told me that the hack came with failsafes. Opening the shunt to the soup of one's neuro-chemical self created ecstasy sure enough, but learning to swim your consciousness through two brain-lakes at once had driven a few pioneers mad.

"You always said you'd leave when you became unhappy," she said quietly.

If we could just get past these words—if Darcy and I could just get a real glimpse. I'd run out of ways to buy time.

"I'm not *that* unhappy," I promised. "Not yet."

I turned the radio back up. Whoever had coded the failsafes into the nano-board had favored alarms; Emil twisted the code into sequences from old AM number stations—the Cold War cryptography that used to fill gaps between broadcasts so covert agents could get their orders remotely, listening and listening for answers. In Emil's mod, these cryptic sequences chanted and squealed if your chem levels started displacing the wrong fluids. The recordings guided Emil's users back into themselves when they tired of or became confused by sharing synaptic data.

Emil had given me a sample chip—the adapter in my transistor played one of the sequences now: *two, five, seven,* a robotic child moaned, now and then swallowed by the theramin squeal of a jamming signal. *Two, Charlie—two.* It sounded like a command.

I hoped Darcy was listening.

"I have an idea," she said.

I tightened my grip

---

on my beer. A painting clung to the wall behind Darcy: some vegetarian-looking thing. A bunch of cows were grazing in this neon field. Dinner forks were sprouting and grabbing the cows by their faces. I thought it was funny. The nearest cow peered suspiciously at four metal nubbins in the grass—a perfect, bovine skeptic. Another cow had been pulled halfway into the earth, and yet another gnawed on a dusty, black fork. Forks and cows peppered the entire field.

Staring at the painting was easier than staring at her.

I wish I had painted it.

"Sorry. This isn't exactly easy," I said.

Darcy grabbed her beer with both hands. "Good. I mean, it would be worse if it was."

Cows and forks. Rank and file. Clarion musak sounded the march.

I stretched my feet under the table. "So, sooner or later?"

She took another sip. "Sooner, it's burning me up."

I fumbled through my jacket and extracted the document carefully—I'd rolled it into a scroll and tied it with a bit of navy ribbon. The pulp-kit and the handful of poached hides I used to counterfeit my parchment had cost as much as the going implant rate—at least, the last I heard about.

Emil had offered the hack for free.

I dusted my hands, and Darcy placed a sheet of folded paper on the table.

Perfect.

I rolled my scroll across the table and came back with her page. At least she had the courtesy to flatten my scroll carefully. I slipped my fingers under her fold and flipped open the terms. No lies. No deals. Just—

No.

—us.

The period was even there, blatant in twelve point Times, perfect in the center of the page.

Perfect.

I stared. "You didn't even . . . you *typed* this."

She lit another cigarette, eyes downcast. I wanted to ring her up—I wanted to do it by thought. God, I needed to know what she was thinking. I couldn't handle this . . . *occlusion* anymore.

I couldn't handle these goddamn words.

"Darcy," my hand found the beer again, "you said . . ."

She feinted a glance at the door. "So did you."

I twisted her paper. "Then what is this?"

She took a long time folding my scroll. She even dragged her nails across the crease so it would make a perfect, wallet-sized memento and brandished it between us before tucking it away.

And the gauntlet rang as it cracked my face.

I felt like those cows on the wall. One of the forks pressed against my temples; I'm surprised I didn't bleed on the table. I couldn't paint this.

"You—wait—"

Two.

Wait, no!

She pulled her relay out.

"Alone, sitting at my desk," she said, "this was much easier."

Five.

Emil's dermoplasts started climbing my brain-stem. I could feel their relay foreman heating up his orders on the back of my neck, unleashing his replicatory proteins into my bloodstream.

Another fork lanced into my eyes.

"Wait!" I ordered.

Seven.

The 'plasts, long since done with smoothing my flesh, turned their enzymes on the relay's data. I could feel the relay itself, under my skin, querying every port of every person's relay stored in my nano-board. The ports were firing too quickly. Everyone noded in, confused and helplessly eavesdropping. The 'plasts knocked a few out, devouring their record on my 'board before transmitting . . . *something.*

"I could do it then, at home," Darcy continued—I could barely hear her. "I just experimented—you know, as if I'd never give it to you. But now," she swallowed, tapping something into her semi-curled relay with a frown, "You're here."

Two, Charlie.

I winced when the 'plasts devoured Darcy's data—I didn't have her port memorized. If I didn't get it again, tonight, I'd never get it back. I'd never get her back.

I sat, watching my cigarette burn. I'd told myself I'd be so much happier if she'd advance. I'd have the clean conscience. I could do what I wanted—what I needed.

Two.

The 'plasts went back to sleep, and my neck stopped burning. I could almost feel my nano-board cooling behind my ears, easing back into itself and the banks upon banks of now-empty partitions. Everyone had disappeared from my relay—I couldn't contact anyone.

Why did we have to write it down?

I read the scroll aloud: "'No.'"

She paused. "Yeah."

"We agreed," I said, rubbing my eyes.

"Yeah."

I didn't say anything. Ultimately, I jammed another cigarette between my lips.

Darcy wriggled into her jacket—that corduroy one I gave her last Christmas.

"Wait."

She turned.

I managed to look at her. "Do you . . . how about more beer?"

A trio of hackers drifted away nearby, smiling and grabbing at each other. I couldn't decide—was I seeing nothing or everything between them?

Darcy followed them out.

The Basement, Borges

I saw an iridescent sphere of almost unbearable brilliance. At first I thought it was revolving; then I realized that this movement was an illusion created by the dizzying world it bounded.

    —Jorge Luis Borges, "El Aleph"

I'M NOT ALLOWED TO KILL ANYONE, NOT TODAY, BUT RIGHT now I have a gun in each hand. One is pointed at Chelsea, and I've got the other pressed against my neck. I've seen too many hostage situations where, in the confusion of the moment, the gunman shoots someone accidentally or, alternately, things go wrong, and he simply opens his own skull in a moment of panic. I figured I'd go ahead and cover both bases.

The rules aren't mine—they come with the gig—but Chelsea doesn't know that, so she stares at the tiny hole at the end of the barrel, seeing it as somehow more potent than anything. I know she feels drawn to it. Like the imagined funnel of a black hole, the barrel gapes at her—a gravity well, its little mouth rounded in shock as if surprised to see her. I recall that black holes resonate in B-flat.

We're sort of comically frozen like this. No one is really sure what to do next, so I think to myself, *What would Borges do?*

Borges shared aleph points with the world after an associate of his discovered one in his basement—a tiny sphere of light. A convergence. One can simply look into an aleph and see everything from subatomic vibration to the swirling of stellar dust— all at once. The universe.

What Borges *didn't* know is that alephs offer enlightenment —I know, I've attained it.

If you can center your head in one, you begin to move with the cosmos. In the early days, when I had trouble enticing people to visit *my* basement—where I, too, found an aleph—I decided I would make a better bodhisattva if I could figure out how to move this aleph around, then I could guide *it* through people's heads, rather than guiding people's *heads* through it.

So I work with bullets. Only the first shot from each of my guns will do the trick—the bullets shove the aleph down the barrel and into my acolyte-to-be. Once you're hit by the universe, a single bullet doesn't do much damage, so in the instants following enlightenment, when my bullets collide with flesh and bone and pissed-off neurons, nothing really happens. Sometimes, scars like stigmata suggest what would have been a lethal shot, but the generation of acolytes I'm creating thinks those are trendy, those stigmata—like enameled labrets or tongue rings, perhaps. They look good under black light and go well with glow sticks.

The other bullets, though, are all business. I've never learned what happens to them, but they're always gone by the time we get home. Pennies for Charon, I suppose.

Anyway, I'm not psychic—I know Chelsea's name because she wears it on her name-tag. She works for a bank—this bank, in fact. I've been watching her for weeks now: where she lives, the car she drives, how she spends her free time, even the soaps in her shower and her favorite detergent. It takes a while to select an acolyte, but Chelsea eats organic food, uses biodegradable soap, and reads books by guys like Weil and Chopra. She's passed all the tests, and today's her day.

"Please," she mutters, a shaking hand pressed against her forehead, "please."

I can only smirk—the neck-gun is tugging on half my face.

"Only a minute more," I tell her.

But I can't wait much longer. Banks like this one keep secret buttons everywhere that scream like molten slag through their security networks. Of course, once these bankers press their secret buttons, I am left with about as much time as it takes to run to the corner market.

Not that I can blame them for pressing those buttons—how good that must feel. Handling money every day, entering data, and going through the other inhuman motions of banking, these tellers have to face the temptation of those emergency buttons as they sit in their little, plastic halls, lifted into dignity by Formica plinths, and like the Pope, shielded with plexiglass.

Chelsea's eyes quiver like puddles of sapphire ink. I can't remember my final thoughts prior to enlightenment, so I wonder what's going through her mind. Somewhere in the dark meat of her brain, synaptic explosions are sending shockwaves through her face and into the aleph—the doorway of light at the end of the barrel. Who knows but her thoughts might be disturbing the clouds of the Horsehead Nebula.

A filament of gold hair flutters before her eyes, and her ruby lips part in sticky realization—a curtain of membranous lip-skin retreats as she gapes her understanding.

B-flat and blood—bullets sing, too. For the briefest instant, as the bullet shoves its aleph into Chelsea's brain, I can hear it harmonize with the black hole in the center of our galaxy. It makes a sound like "Om."

I swing my other gun in a great, benedictory arc past the other people on the bank's floor. Chelsea blinks at me, her sapphire eyes like white-hot stars, and I help her up. I can hear guns firing—the police must have arrived—but right on cue, my portal appears, and pain like flashfire erupts behind my eyes. I walk Chelsea into the darkness, and we leave the gunfire behind. A different memory hides in each of these getaways, and this time it's a flash image of a birthday cake. White frosting and rainbow edges—it sits on a harvest gold countertop, and my mother wears her hair like a hippie.

———

Our journey, of course, was strange—blood misted and loud, gunshots belching like unpleasant ideas. How are these portals possible? Wormholes—tubes like pneumatic shafts with which our universe courts its neighbors, sending salutations, love poems, and letters of regret in the languages of radiation and density. You find them in black holes, where anything is everything else.

Chelsea is sitting on one of my stolen couches, watching television for the first time through her enlightened eyes, the remote control in one hand, a dampened beer in the other. She offered her clothes without protest when I asked for them—like mine, they'd been soiled in transit. They tumble together now in the gray soup of my washing machine, where the final drops of her normality disappear. She looks good in one of my shirts, her nondescript underwear peering shyly from beneath. She'll be loyal, this one—not one of the aloof enlightened, afraid of her own navel and chewing funereal dust.

"We'll be on the news soon," she calls, eyes locked on the television.

I laugh. "We're always on the news—it happens every time. You'll get used to the attention."

The couch's previous owner hadn't looked as good sitting like that. I move furniture, and sometimes I'm able to blend business with pleasure. The day before I enlightened that woman, I spent hours with unnamed day-workers wrestling armoires and dinettes between sheetrock walls, suffering smears like whitewash upon all the salient points of my body. We lifted endtables over Travertine landscapes and watched our footing over Berber savannahs. I can remember the texture of my partner's face, pressed together, as we had been, by the angles of the woman's beautiful oriel-window staircase. Our unshaven chins abraded one another, making noise like cricketsong for animals with good ears.

Moving the couch a second time, later that night, we had strained our muscles without sound, just as careful as before, disemboweling her home. I believe that woman works downtown now, near the interstate and its federal cemetery—staying close, I'd assume, to the death she's conquered. I see her reports on billboards there—the too-neat penmanship in greasepaint graffiti, informing me in vulgar hieroglyphs how she's handling enlightenment. Her end tables are in my bedroom.

Chelsea waves me into the living room, and I join her on the couch. Her thigh is cool against my leg, limned in blue moonlight. Her flesh, unlike mine, is pliable—it gives ever so gracefully. The air is cold when I inhale, and I have to struggle against the recession of my thoughts, the decay of cognition by which women reduce me to barely-thinking meat.

"We look old," Chelsea says, her blue eyes glowing.

I'm not looking at the television—I've seen these reports before. "Everything is old to a security camera—it doesn't see well, and the images it remembers will expire by tomorrow, when its audience looks instead for traffic reports and consumer warnings."

"It looks like a zoetrope," she states, condensation from her beer pooling upon her thigh. I'm staring anxiously as this water collects moonlight—soon it will weep onto my own flesh.

"A what?" I ask, uninterested. I can see darkness and city lights honeycombed in that water, which, like an amoeba, extends itself in silvery arcs across her skin, leaking in one direction toward my own flesh, and in the other toward Chelsea's curious undergarments. She will want to remove them soon.

"A zoetrope," she repeats. "Children spin them. There are drawings inside."

Watching the infinitude of tiny lights in the water on Chelsea's leg, I squeeze her shoulder, heart pounding. I consider my allies: enlightened men who haven't felt the pliability of cold flesh for hundreds of years. Iskander Zu al-Karnayn, listed in the Borges report, first owned the crystal mirror that reflects the entire world—the entire borrowing of lights invoked in rainwater, ocean waves, or wet skin. Tariq ibn-Ziyad, in *Thousand and One Nights*, found the reflection in a tower. Water shimmered like an aleph for Merlin in *The Faerie Queene*—I can quote it: "round and hollow . . . and seem'd a world of glas"—he called it his "universal mirror."

"You can't tell who we are," Chelsea interrupts, her skin now thoroughly limned in the liquid glow of a beer-water aleph. Like my allies, I can see the entire universe in that quivering light, I can imagine all things.

"They're calling it a massacre."

I relax my grip. "So would you."

She still hasn't moved.

"Nine people shot and not a dollar stolen."

I finally glance at the screen. "No one knows how to describe a bodhisattva at work."

Borges knew the truth; he said, "The Faithful who gather at the mosque of Amr, in Cairo, are acquainted with the fact that the entire universe lies inside one of the stone pillars that ring its central court . . . No one, of course, can actually see it . . ."

Of course they can't—an aleph locked in a pillar enlightens no one.

I finally turn off the television, and the lights upon her leg scatter. There is moonlight, in places, but the aleph has fled—it will await me again in the basement. We are finished, for now, with the business of infinite lights and singing holes —the washing machine has drained the last of her blood. The aurora glow of drifting nebulae can't see us just now, and there are comets resuming their tasks, thinking no longer of Chelsea, but of long, long orbits that, despite the illusion of straight-line travel, will eventually curve back to the beginning.

I remove the rest of Chelsea's clothes, feeling everywhere the motions of her skin. Borges would have done so, had Beatriz still lived, but, observant as he was, the man couldn't see how the lights of the universe can animate the dead.

She makes a sound like "Om," my Chelsea. How she moves so much, sitting still with her pliable skin.

Slipstring

'VE WANTED, SINCE THE BEGINNING, TO WALK THESE CARNIVAL roads. I've craved the aromatic pinch of body odor and funnel cake, and I enjoy the massage of errant palms in Midway crowds. More importantly, I suppose, I know the owners: the chimes of touch-screens and ski-ball fill ledgers of code in my office, but I compose—I do not listen. Before now, I have only known how the key of C looks. It is prettier than it sounds.

Buffeted by thermal ghosts and burning canvas, I catch splashes of the inferno as it slops through the park. I can only assume all of this is a result of the chemicals I used to start the fire. Or maybe it's this string—it's altered everything.

Three days ago, I awoke to the string. Across the duvet, along the carpet, and through the door—the string came from someplace outside. It had embedded itself in my chest and begun to tug. I didn't panic—I merely got out of bed and obeyed the tugging. Putting on my bra proved strange with the string in the way. I decided on a button-down to save myself the same trouble with a shirt.

I know this inferno—I have designed it for years in program after program. I can hear its harmonics in the shouts of its victims, and I realize now that I should have paid attention sooner. Certainly there are sparks between the lines of my work, but at least the string has led me here. I've wandered and jogged and waited for days, going as the string bid me, going when it tugged, meandering through urban labyrinths. I have seen no minotaurs. My name is Joey.

That first morning, the string led me to un-interesting places: a diner, the drycleaners, a pay-to-park parking lot, a bench. The string only extended about twenty feet, stiff, pulsating like some psychedelic phallus. It is thin, barely the diameter of a segment of yarn—it is not fuzzy. No one else saw it protruding from my chest, but Michael could see the little skin-temple answering its tug.

There was a space between us—like magnetic repulsion—but the moonlight had grabbed our bare asses with pastel fingertips and shoved—didn't cease to shove—so we lay, naked and not touching. He circled his fingertips around little skin temple—it quivered in tiny, delighted shakes, and the string danced to avoid his touch.

This could be something, he said. An abscess, or a tumor—you know, something dangerous.

My finger touched it readily. No, it's just the tugging.

What's tugging on you?

The string, I said.

What string?

I rolled my eyes. The glowing one protruding from my chest.

Oh, he said. That one.

This is taking me places. I'm not drifting anymore—I'm going where I'm bid, no wandering.

Does it matter where you're led? he asked.

Not really, I said. It's not the space you inhabit but how you fill it. I touched his crotch—he had only the one normal lump thereabouts. Here we are, all geared up, but you prefer the space. That's fine, but this is a different use of nudity and moonlight. I've been led here as a lover; you're here to write poetry about it later.

He smiled.

I'll go elsewhere for my pleasure, you know.

I know.

<hr>

So I program computers—or used to: load script. Run. There is an office downtown, a nice one with glass walls and green sculpture. It is in the middle of other nice offices with glass walls and green sculpture: Emerald Park—a suite of office spaces, crypt upon crypt of aging mainframes and lurking e-servers. It might better be called the Emerald City: Each tower comes with its own wizard—a little man with tremendous resources and works of art on his extra office tables. When I was told how to go home and why, I clicked my heels and smiled. I have money still—it's folding and decaying in nonexistent spasms, in infinitesimal hiccups in the mainframes of other lands. Bigger wizards dictate how, and I will grow old in the manner they deem best. Load meaning. It had been my job to correct errors between product releases.

Michael's house had been my last stop that first day, so I lied with him for hours, the moonlight thrumming along my upright string. I no longer cared for the empty glass on his nightstand, the one another lover used two years prior. He hadn't touched her either, but he still preserved the artifacts of her presence. There barely remained any of the gloss with which she had ghosted a kiss onto the glass.

He kept other things crucial for his poet's distance: books he hadn't read, a collection of fine liquors, a cache of digital pornography.

I left the next day before dawn. The string pulled, and I followed. I didn't walk far, just to my car. As I drove, the string dipped and swung, fingering like an angry needle the directions it wanted. After a time, I deposited my car in a garage. Back in the sunshine, I didn't have to wait long to find my first person. I sat with him on a bench smeared with an advertisement for advertising on benches. Backup. Load bench.

Where are you going in such a hurry? he asked.

I'm not in a hurry. File: replace. I just know where I'm going.

Where's that, he asked?

I didn't want him to ask.

Delete.

I'm not in a hurry. I just know where I'm going.

Where's that?

Safemode.

I'm going to the Fair Grounds, to the Fair.

Shall I come along, he asked. He held a paper cup wrapped in a trademarked sleeve of corrugated cardboard—I could see the trademark between his fingers. The no-spill space dome lidding the cup had become lined with spokes of spilled coffee. There was, around the valved opening, a ring of coffee—wet and dirty. I thought of Michael's pornography.

You'll have to come because it's the right thing to do, I said. I mean, it feels to you the correct thing to do at the moment, and you have to leave only when you realize you have nothing better to do.

Yeah, sure. He smiled.

He needed to go home and erase himself. He had spilled his directory all over himself, and I could see it. It was obscene. I decided a little reduction was in order.

—␣—

Delete.

—␣—

I knew where I was going, and this arthouse bum wanted to come along. I was happy to have him—shiny watch and all.

He was the other guy, the pleasure. Todd. I saw him regularly. And I knew we weren't going to the Fair. Tonight was Friday, which meant Todd would be going to the arena. I don't like wrestling, but I like Todd, and the string seemed to also.

He found a beer as we walked—I didn't notice how, but I watched as he emptied his coffee cup and refilled it with the can. He swallowed what wouldn't fit beneath the lid.

The arena offered only the sounds of its audience. I expected loud music, wandering lights, bikinis. People stood and drank, chattering in one corner about IRAs and about a new syndicate in another. My string fluttered, waggling its vaporous tail around the jaws of the people nearby. I waited for it to stiffen and jerk, but I was awarded only a pain in my chest and a film of sweat on my neck:

That one over there, Todd said, is the queen.

Of what?

This place. Every week, her goons roll that damned throne out, and she slides into it, jugs of corner-mart cola tucked under each arm.

And her hair is always teal?

Yep. And always the same shoes, same fuschia nails. Once, she dressed like a fairy, but her boys there, Lancelot and Galahad, they always look like well-greased apartment trash.

I wondered about the difference between apartment and trailer trash.

Have you ever talked to her? I asked

The string was getting excited.

Name's Loni, he said. I think she's with Cain.

I didn't know who that was.

I studied her throne. It could easily seat two people, and it reminded me of the telescoping lounge chairs that scoop parents' asses at Pee-Wee soccer games.

Did she pay for that spot? I asked. How do Lancelot and Galahad keep people out of it?

Todd just looked at me—Some things are understood, Joey.

I knew it—the string convulsed and slapped itself across Loni's face. The queen, in her majesty, paid no attention.

I'm going.

Matches haven't started yet, Todd said.

No. I'm going to sit in that chair. The string has decided.

What string? He swallowed more beer—I had pulled the cool expression from his face.

Goddammit. This one. The one protruding from my chest.

Todd stared.

I fluttered my eyes, but the string lost patience with an angry heave.

We're not fucking tonight, you know that? Todd called. Christ, I'm gonna get Michael in here.

When I stepped up to the queen, the string coiled itself around her chest. Its terminal filaments sparked as they combed her hair.

I need to sit in the throne, I said, bowing.

Who are you?

Get out of the chair.

The throne's braces relented with a good kick, and the canvas supporting Loni sucked into itself. She looked like she'd fallen into a camp latrine. Lancelot and Galahad simply stared.

She screamed, flailing, but the effort only rewarded her more sucking—the throne had now pressed her chest against her knees and was on its way over. She had a lisp.

Let's go, Todd said. The string recoiled and lashed itself onto his arms. I could hear him apologizing as he carried me out.

Take me to the Ferris Wheel.

The string likes the Fair Grounds. It whips and sways and demands directions. By the time we got there, Michael had arrived.

Where's the cab? Todd asked.

On its way, Michael said.

He wouldn't look at me.

Things really have gotten better, I offered, since the string came.

Yeah. Todd sighed, looking back at the lane near the gate where other cabs were gathering, waiting for fares. Let's get her on the damn wheel.

I smiled. No problem. It doesn't close 'til midnight.

They ignored me, and Todd dragged me by the arm toward the Ferris Wheel.

Only one thing, I said—the string seemed happy—take me by that snack tent.

Todd changed direction. Beside him, Michael lit another cigarette.

You bring money? Todd asked.

Yeah.

All right, here, Todd snapped, swiveling his head—I gasped when the string stiffened and pierced him through the eyes.

What?

I swallowed.

Nothing. Give me a smoke.

He did—Last favor—and lit it.

When I opened the helium tank, Michael wasn't fast enough to get the cigarette from my hand. The tank gagged and wheezed, belching glops of fire and a string-tight lance of blue flame. Todd had already started running; Michael paused for only a second. I winked at him as I kicked over the tank. The tent went quickly from there.

They are all running. Todd's gone—Michael left me here. I belong here, with the wheel of fire creaking overhead, the tents hovering on their own flames. The burning people. I can't seem to awaken the string. I stand and tug, the string's dead weight spilling across my fingers. I tug and tug, but there's nowhere left to go. Tugging myself is painful, but I need somewhere to go.

'Seng,
Running

*L*AST NIGHT I WATCHED A DOCUMENTARY ABOUT THE MOON. How it pulls at the oceans. How when it catches its next meteorite, at just the right size, and throws moonrocks like missiles at the upper atmosphere, it will cause a disaster. Tsunamis and hurricanes and push-pull tides that won't let any of it go. The Eastern Seaboard, and England, will both be underwater.

My yard looks like this, like the surface of the moon. There are craters and ridges and little mountains of dirt everywhere—front and back. Some are peaked, the freshest spots, from the last time I pulled. When there was still ginseng to pull. We haven't had enough rain to wash down the dirt, and now, with the fat moonlight everywhere on the drive and the yard and the curling roof shingles, it looks like my yard is throwing itself at the moon. Instead of the other way around, like they say on the show.

Of course, I'm in the way, getting thrown, too. Already, the disaster is peeling the paint, in places, from the siding. Ours is a modular home, not mobile—they halved it together, from two trucks. A gift from Josie's dad.

The seam, though, could've used stronger bolts, and Josie's dad's men didn't have them. It's a little open, in places.

There isn't a blade of grass in either yard, just the ripped-up dirt all across the firebreak to the paw paws and serviceberries and hemlock trees. Ropes of Virginia creeper are dead like snakes in places at the edge.

On my porch, I can smell a bit of Lake Chisolm. Sloshing, no doubt, in the big moonrays. Like they said on the show. There's no ginseng there, either. It's already all been pulled—by me and some others, mostly last year. Six hundred dollars a pound, to the Chinese. And they can tell the wild from the domestic. Domestic's not worth anything. I had to transplant a few and let them set like weeds, on their own, just to get some roots from my own yard.

Josie has the last of our stash inside. She's making 'seng tea and pudding for Shell. Shell's been sick a month, and there's nothing left in our line of credit. No room on the cards. No more loans against the title and the checkbook. There's nothing but the fever, and the runs, and the pains in her joints. She cries when I bend them.

Inside, Josie's skin looks as gray as Shell's. She sleeps in snatches on her folded arms, her fingers working at the peeling laminate on the kitchen table. Working. Picking and rolling. Over and over. Like she's cleaning 'seng. One root at a time, a nap at a time. Ten minutes, that's all. She looks like she's forty. Last month, we both turned twenty-four.

"She needs a clean diaper," Josie says.

I pull one out of the half-torn plastic under the sink. A few semi-translucent slices of already-steeped 'seng cling like slugs to the tile. When I'm finished with Shell, I'll take them out onto the porch, where they can dry in tomorrow's sun. I'll re-use them, the next time me and Josie can get a quiet hour. When we're both awake enough to put on the radio and slip into the bedroom.

"You going senging?" Josie asks.

"Nowhere to go," I say. I inspect the contents of Shell's used diaper before tying it in a grocery bag and sealing it in the diaper-bin.

Josie lights a cigarette at the table, waiting on the kettle. On the 'seng. If we can just keep enough around, we can take care of Shell.

With her off-hand, Josie toys with our last whole root, running her fingers up and down its legs. They look like little, deformed men, the roots. Usually without heads.

"Nothing on Darrel's scanner?" Josie asks. The radio spits music faintly from the counter. I realize that it's been on the entire time. Some song about kicking ass, about American boots in Pakistani caves. It's a stupid song, but Josie likes it.

"No."

Darrell's scanner picks up police and ranger stations. When people are poaching, we know, and we follow a few days later. Sometimes we collect the 'seng they couldn't get away with.

I tap the tape-tabs into place on Shell's little hips. A few weeks ago, she'd been jaundiced, as yellow as a sink-washed 'seng root. Now she is only gray. I touch her lips when she puckers them at me.

I look at Josie. She needs to wash her hair.

"I'll drive to Mason," I say. "I'll talk to Darrell in Mason."

In Mason, in the bar, they're playing that same stupid song. Kicking Arab ass. America. Electric guitars. Some line about pie. People are nodding over their light beers and smoking along.

The windows in this place are blacked against the moonlight. Outside, there are two tail pipes for every truck, growling and choking as people come and go. Trailer hitches dangling truck-sized, rubber testicles. Mason is an important place. For everybody.

Darrell is sitting at the bar, the heels of his boots hooked onto the stool's cross-bars. There's a football game on three different TVs overhead.

I sit beside him.

"Hey."

He exaggerates a smile. "Hey, Troy."

The bartender sets a beer down in front of me—the same kind as always. Darrell watches, his eyes behind the lines of the bartender's overtight tank top.

I take my time lighting a cigarette, waiting for her to walk away.

"Anything on the scanner?"

Darrell looks back at the game. "No."

Someone cheers himself at the pool table. Screaming. A dickhead like the rest.

"Anybody saying anything?" I ask.

Darrell drinks. He's single. No kids. Works at a silo outside Cascade. To him, 'senging means new guns, a better blind, an ounce of weed, maybe. To him, it's just machismo in the woods, playing army. Sneaking around the sinkholes and inside the caves, pulling 'seng when he can. Looking for something to beat up or shoot at or even just run from.

He's rough with the 'seng. Gouging it out of the soil, and cramming it into his fists. He always calls them *little fuckers*, the roots, and stares at them like they're little, brown people.

"No."

I watch the game with him.

"How's Shell?" he asks.

"Same."

"Doctor say?"

I pick at the label on the beer. "Can't take her."

After a while, he stares at his bottle. Finally, some Williams on the stereo. Something decent.

"You might could poach with Evan," Darrell says.

I look at him. "Yeah? When?"

"Whenever."

"Sunday?"

"Yeah."

We drink with Evan sometimes, but we don't 'seng with him. Not normally. Never wanted to. He pulls like an idiot, at Mammoth Cave, running right around the rangers and the photoreactive dyes—even the tourists camping around the caves. Sometimes, I think he even lives in one.

I don't have much choice.

"I'll tell him," Darrell said. "Bring that .38."

"Pawned it," I said.

"Beretta, then."

I don't say anything.

I've been caught before. Not at Mammoth Cave, but on a reserve. It wasn't hunting season, and there hadn't been anybody for weeks. It was good there, but, at the end of a ranger's winking gun barrel, I emptied my pockets, surrendered my rifle, and went along. I sold Josie's Olds to pay the fine. Only three months in jail. Then probation.

And never a job again. Not at the plant, not at the silos, not even at the drive-through.

I move to the left a little, reel in the jig, and recast. I could care less if there are any crappie beneath the fallen cypress alongside this pier, but it needs to look like I'm doing something. Like I have a good reason for being around the park so late. Here, and around Chisolm, you can do anything, so long's you're fishing.

Moths and may flys swarm dumbly around the goose-necked pier lights. The yellowed insect bulbs make rows of artificial moons on the water. The real one is behind the clouds tonight.

Further down the pier, some people are talking in the fishing house. I stare at it. Not going in. In Texas, around Opossum Kingdom Lake, Josie's grandfather stumbled into one drunk. he hit his head against the bar, then went out cold. Then into the fishing hole. He died face down in a four-foot square of lakewater, a copy of Aristotle in his plumber's-shirt pocket. Those others, in there now, don't even know books can sometimes fit in pockets. I don't know why they fish in there. There's plenty of the same water out here, where people like me can help if something happens.

But those houses are for doing things alone in public places. Like reading books on a fishing pier. Like drowning for it.

Evan finally shows up, his footsteps hammering onto the pier. I reel the jig out of the water and run my fingers across its chenille torso, across the goggled lead eyes. Really, it's too dark for the lure to make any sort of difference.

Evan spits over the rail as he steps up, his bottom lip puffed with tobacco. He waves at a man on the other end and settles his forearms beside mine.

"Hey, Evan."

"Troy," he says. He arranges his tobacco with his tongue. The lights along the pier can't find his eyes under the rim of his hat. He fiddles absently with the knife on his belt.

"How's fish?" he asks.

"Yeah," I say. "Fine. Got a reel?"

He spits again. "At home."

We stand silently for a time. Everywhere around us, tree frogs and crickets saw at the night air. A few Silver-Haired bats flutter past the big lights over our heads. The trees are nothing but stippled, dark places. At night, they never have names—not unless the moon's out, splashing all everything.

But one day, it could be chunks of screaming hot meteorites, and not slow, Kentucky moon beams. One day, there'll be a disaster.

"How well you know the park?" Evan asks.

"Been around a few times."

"You get your guns back?"

I look at him. "Can I borrow one of yours?"

"Yeah."

He pulls the brim of his hat lower over his eyes. Pushes it back up. Settles it back again at the beginning.

"Five pounds," he says. "That's all is good right now."

I remember to cast the line again, watching as the new ripples in the still water slam the artificial moons into each other.

"Yeah. All right."

Shell is sleeping tonight. Josie looks at her occasionally, in her padded crib, under the built-in desk where we keep the dvds. Shell hasn't filled as many diapers today. Her stool is firming. When I squat down and look at her through the daisy-printed mesh, her pallor looks purple, splashed by the TV light. She doesn't look as blue as she does in her room because the window is on the other side of the living room. The moonlight is on the other side.

Josie has the TV turned down. She's watching the celebrity news channel, her arms folded across her chest.

Back in the kitchen, I have the first new root in my hand. It's heavy, at least a quarter of a pound, even after we steeped and mashed one of its legs for Shell.

Josie and I haven't had sex in weeks. I don't even think either of us has showered in two days. It doesn't matter. I cut a coin of 'seng from the root with my buck knife and eat it. I cut three more, peel back the knotty, brown skin, and drop them into a glass with two cubes of ice. I fill it with Wabash Corn Whiskey.

Josie sees it in my hand when I join her on the couch. For a long time, we make a game of not being too forward. We stare at, chuckle with, and ridicule the celebrity news quietly. Eventually, I finish the whiskey, swallow the 'seng, and move in on Josie. We paw and tickle and fuss for half an hour. Even now, Josie still looks tired.

But there's no erection. I eat more 'seng, chewing it harder and swallowing it slower. But Josie takes Shell into her room and sleeps. Outside, I stare at the moonlight and the sweetgum trees.

Evan meets me outside the cave. It's near a smaller sinkhole far enough away from the named and toured entrances in the proper part of the park. I look past him, looking for a stove, or a sleeping bag, or a door made from trees, but it's too dark to see anything. When I was a Boy Scout, the troop would hike through some of these, before any of us had heard of 'seng. Before any went to jail, got married, went to college. Some went to college.

One time, we had spent hours scraping at our flints-and-steel, creating piles of filed magnesium and lighting them with our waterproof matches. The flames had been pink, and they hissed while we stared. We told the scoutmaster that we were burning potato chips, and he left us alone. Terry called Tommy gay, 'cause he liked the pink fires. There was a fight after Tommy pissed on him. Tommy quit after that.

Evan hands me a .22 pistol. He's bored down the barrel and made a silencer by stuffing washers into a new casing.

He pulls his brim over his eyes. Looking around, he lifts it back up, and settles it again at the beginning. He has an ultraviolet flashlight in his hand.

"Anything on the scanner?" he asks.

The scanner is Darrell's. I have no idea.

"No."

"Good. How's the rangers?"

I shrug. "Quiet."

He starts hiking, red LED flashlight in one hand, ultraviolet in the other. We'll use the gun if we scare up any bobcats.

I have to drive to Louisville to make a sale—up 31 past Fork Knox and through West Point. Things are very clean just before Louisville.

I park the Ford near a loading dock behind Broadway, between the Chickasaw and Shawnee Parks. My guy, Randy, runs a head shop and apothecary from an upstairs front. He's in the alley beneath the fire escape, spray painting glass mirrors black. Inside, he sells them as dark mirrors to the New Agers.

He looks up briefly, a cloud of black paint wafting through the braids in his beard.

"Hey, Troy."

I've got my hands in my pockets.

"Hey, Randy. Business?"

He frog-waddles over to another mirror without standing up. "Same. Been 'senging?"

I look around. At the far end of the alley, between two refurbished brick facades, day shoppers pass in and out of view, plastic-handled shopping bags between them.

"Yeah."

"Seven hundred a pound," Randy says, picking a Sassafrass twig off the newly wet mirror. A few of them blow in sometimes from Shawnee Park. The alley is scabbed with their leaves.

I watch him for a minute. Offering seven hundred means he's hoping I haven't heard how good the market is this month. He knows I don't really sell much place else.

It's enough, though.

"That much?" I play along. "Let's go upstairs."

In his workroom, I can only half-hear the bagpipes and synthesizers he's playing through his stereo. Wafts of Nag Champa curl through the bead curtain on the opposite wall. He zeros out his scales and takes the roots when I hand them to him. Only a pound. Me and Josie and Shell need the rest.

When he's finished, he puts the roots in a black-painted box, plugs the thing in, and throws its blackout skirt over his head. He studies the roots through a hole, looking for the Ag Department's dyes. These days, they paint the 'seng against these sorts of things. When they can find it.

I stand around dumbly, waiting. He's polite when he pulls the roots out, flips on his metal detector, and waves them under its paddle. I'm glad there aren't any tracking pins in these roots. I wasn't sure.

Satisfied, Randy unlocks his counter-safe, sandalwood beads swinging around his neck. He tucks the roots inside and pulls out a stack of bills. I can see his .44 on the little safe's top shelf.

"Put another coat on those mirrors while you're down," he says.

Evan is quiet while I pull. He stands against a tree, his lights turned off for now. The ultraviolet didn't find any dyes on this plant, so I'm being careful, digging out the soil in the broken moonlight. Digging by feel. I don't really need to see.

I cut the root out with my buck knife and jam the severed trunk back into the soil. It'll die just the same, but just in case. In case a ranger comes along. This'll buy another day or two.

I hand the pistol to Evan and wrap the root in a chamois. We've got most of five pounds now. Around us, the wind rattles things, upsetting a screech owl some fifty yards off or so. The aromas of turned earth and witchhazel are ghosting around us. The mosquitoes are bad this year, whining amongst themselves as they explore our ears.

Evan kneels suddenly, hissing in reverse as he sucks in his breath. "Don't move."

All the 'seng is piled in its chamois by his heel.

"Stay where you are," a bullhorn commands. A floodlight is painting the surrounding trees, trying to find us. It gets Evan's hat for a second. My heart is pumping bile through my veins, and I'm not moving. I'm thinking about running, my eyes on the moon-splattered 'seng. My eyes are on Shell, on Josie's hair. On the gap between the two halves of our house.

Evan leans into the 'seng and whispers, his fingers tugging on the brim of his hat. The flood throws another searching parallelogram of light across the black oaks around us.

"Step into the light!" the bullhorn barks. I can't tell how many of them there are.

Evan spits when he's done. When he's done the whispering. Darrel would've just thrown them. He would have been angry at the roots and the caves they landed in. Not the ranger. He would have made conversation with the ranger.

The piled 'seng roots stand up quickly, shrugging away my chamois like they're slipping out of bed. Standing on their hairy, root-legs, they look headlessly around for a minute and then run away. They run into the dappled shadows, staying close on their needled toes to shrub-stalks and undergrowth, hiding from the night watchers like the screech owls and the bobcats.

The flood finds me before it gets Evan, and I can hear the ranger cock his shotgun.

Evan sets the brim of his hat again, lifts his doctored .22, and shoots. It hiccups quietly, and the flood looks elsewhere.

The 'seng has run itself away. I have only the two warty, unmarketable roots in my pocket. For no good reason, I run after Evan as he jogs toward the fallen floodlight.

He hit the ranger in the chest. The shotgun is lying beside his canted legs, and he's breathing heavily, staring, and he slaps dumbly at the wound. Me and Evan chop up my warty 'seng on a chunk of slate and shove it into the wound. We shove and shove, but it isn't enough. It can't do for the ranger what it can't do for Shell.

At home, I park the Ford and climb out stiffly. I walk mechanically across the yard, across the peaks and divots and disrupted soil. I'm going after it all with the hose and rake tomorrow. I'm going to smooth everything out.

Josie takes the money when I hand it to her on the couch.

One root is big enough, the biggest one, so I set it down and whisper. I tell it to walk.

It walks across the living room. Shell isn't in her crib anymore, so the 'seng climbs over the daisy-printed mesh and settles inside. It kicks its legs, moving purple freckles across its hoary skin where the TV shines through the mesh.

Fairyland

ALILEE," Cap said, turning toward the house. He'd stood still, watched Gil from the moment they dropped him off.

"Where is 'Galilee?'" Gil asked.

Cap stopped. Squinted against the sun.

"It's here for sure," he said. "Long way that direction and that. A long way in all directions."

Gil looked at the sun, too, but he did not squint. He was blind to it now. It was cooler, easier to see than the explosion at ground zero. Where the air itself had incandesced. A phosphor haze. A *séideán sídhe* pushing gamma rays and X-rays and blackbody radiation over three counties.

"Galilee's not a farm," Cap said.

"Where am I?" Gil asked.

———

A valley. Pastures, which had gone bad. Empty. Haze obscured the surrounding hills. It was what Gil had expected of The Bomb. An Indian Summer twinkling radioactive ejecta. Refracting sunbeams like farm dust or smog. Or burning magnesium. He thinks of his own ghosts, and wonders if they burned up somewhere else, in the past. Maybe the whole world was dead already. Maybe we were all eaten up and spat out in radioactive chunks.

———

"They use tattoos to tell you apart," Gil said.

Cap lit a cigarette. "Yes."

"How many of you are there?" Gil asked.

Cap smoked, measuring Gil over his knuckles.

"Few thousand, best I can tell."

Cap tossed a pack of cigarettes onto the table. Gil didn't see an ashtray. They smoked for a while, the fridge chugging in the corner.

"This isn't all of it," Cap said. He slipped the bandana off his head. Tattooed along his brow, and into the cords of his remaining hair, an ivy circlet wreathed the top of his face.

"They'll pick something for you. They'll give you a story."

Cap leaned away. The kitchen's swamp light shone in his eyes.

"Why do you call it 'Galilee?'" Gil asked.

Emptiness. The sound of beer bottles. Nothing.

He followed Cap, looked again at the contrail—the fairy wind had feathered it. A cloud now, a cirrus ribbon that might be nothing more than it seemed.

Cap planted the crate on the ground and tore free its chute.

"Who makes these drops?" Gil said.

"They do," Cap said, digging through a stack of canned beef. He tossed a can at Gil, tore open a carton of cigarettes, and started cramming things into his pockets.

"Hungry?" Cap said.

"Sure," Gil said.

"Well, eat up."

"Where are we going?"

"Work to do," Cap said.

Gil didn't argue.

He had seen all of this before. He cut his thumb on the edge of the can's lid. Oiled gravy lipped the tin's razor edge, and the fluid ran in curls down Gil's finger, displaced by his blood and unwilling to mix. Gil shook his hand clean. Waited for his blood to become things like soil, and grass, and clusters of mint.

Cap reminded Gil of his grandfather—both men were short. Gil's grandfather had kept his military insignia in a shadow-box.

It was among the possessions They confiscated from Gil. He'd thought about sweating men in the Pacific Rim. Men grown old, who played catch and knew the meanings of words.

Gil had thought about these things. Staring at blueprints and reading recipes that called for potassium chloride and sodium bicarbonate. Glycerin and woodmeal and fistfuls of shrapnel. He hadn't been alone. Before.

Make kaputt what makes you kaputt.
Exactly.

He looked at the wall. From one sketch to another: they were all of her, looking this way, looking that. Some outlined her figure; others sketched only the curve of her spine.

After They arrested him, Gil found out that he and his allies had been mythified too. A code name for whom to chase around the country, around their "Atlantis"—They'd called them Tommyknockers.

Gil took another look at the banister, at the arrangement of its drawings. They climbed the chipped balusters in spirals, doubling back on themselves and climbing. Simultaneously. Cap's noise, from the kitchen, reached Gil dully, as if underwater. In Minthe's river, perhaps.

Gil started tracking the pictures' climb in thirds: over one, over one, up one—back one, down one, over one. Over, over, over—

The man on the wheel, always spinning, arms wide, arrayed in thirds, in spirals—

—in the sequence. 0, 1, 1 . . .

Gil blinked. 2s and 5s flapped through his concentration, migrating elsewhere. You can measure blast radii best with the Golden Mein. With Fibonacci's Numbers. With any aesthetic scale.

———

A glimpse of her breasts. The sketches had been done in ink, with watercolors, charcoal. Some crosshatched, some stippled. Some without lines at all.

———

Cap would teach Gil, They'd told him, on the old county highway behind him, before They pulled the gunny sack off his head and snipped his restraints. They disappeared, federally, down the highway, which had some designation, an alphanumeric code, something hieratic. A holdover from Before, when here had still been a county—still had people and zip codes and residential zoning. Before it became a better place. For people, like Gil, who didn't belong there.

———

And they were everywhere. Gil could see into Cap's parlor: the same dun-colored mosaic, walls and furniture papered with the woman's image. A few of her were impaled on a coat rack, its brazen fingers piercing her eyes, her heart. Hanging from the ceiling fan. A mosaic on the window.

They
Would
Only
Be
Roads

RESTER FINGERED THE CHAIN—HE'D PULLED IT FROM THE
tank behind one of the commodes downtown, in Idio, the
old feed-mill turned nightclub near the depot. The chain
had absorbed such faith in the dank water, pulling endlessly as
expected—as the clubbers believed it would. Prester imagined
each flushing synapse exhausting its neural blast all the way
through the chain and into the water, where it rippled gently
into the lime-scarred porcelain. Idio's clubbers had no doubt
empowered the chain to degrees that, no matter how he found his
gnosis, Prester would never fully measure. The tarnished scars on
the delicate chain's aged links reminded him of flowers, complete
with rusted stems and lines of calcium like pale roots.

He took a deep breath as he eased out of his reverie, now
acutely aware of his apartment's water-stained breath. With a
cough, he eased the chain back into his pocket—it had invaded
his thoughts with decay enough for now.

"I'm going to need more charms," he said aloud, the phosphor
glow of his computer monitor rendering his fingers blue.

"aLan," he called.

The screen on his link-pad blinked at his elbow, its colors
momentarily negative as the slender machine stirred awake.

Prester glanced at it. "Sorry, thought you were in the box."

Lacking speakers to respond, the pad blinked its patience as
Prester linked it up to his stationary computer.

"You set?" Prester asked after a moment.

"I'm here," aLan's androgynous voice said.

"I need more charms," Prester told it. "A *lot* more."

aLan thought for a moment, its status bar slipping across the
monitor's screen. "You have two hundred inactive," it reported.

Prester looked at the diagram tacked to his wall. The newsprint
had yellowed in the last six months, and the storms that had

softened the city last weekend had curled its edges. In lines of colors, twisting, arranged in Solomonic sigils, yoked together by strands of brittle yarn, his ready charms littered the page: names, addresses, e-mail servers—they all promised power in different guises. Some signified chain letters still sleeping in his filing cabinet; others were acronyms for the various forwards in his e-mail inbox. A few were rumors he hadn't yet started. Each carried its own charm, the granted wish it promised for spreading it around. Prester didn't have enough —not to make this new rite capable of generating the wishes it would need. He needed at least enough to diffuse the Levites' anger, should an uninvited wish or two slip past the protective rite and into their sanctum. Prester didn't care what it was they wanted so badly to secure—he just wanted their money.

"No good," he finally concluded. "I already set most of them in the rite: counter-charms." He scratched his head. "And I need the few spares to get out of here later."

aLan did some more thinking. As familiars went, it was slow, but Prester had counted on it for so long, he didn't want to summon a new one—not with today's risks on the web. There was too much at stake now to open himself up to whatever strange programs would answer his call.

"Taylor," aLan eventually reported, "has released eighty charms in the last five days."

Prester wheeled away from the computer, the chair's hissing casters sighing his frustration. With enough active to release that many so quickly, Taylor wouldn't surrender any for cheap.

But what had she done with them?

———

"Why do you need so many?" Taylor asked. The Pipeline was making something digitally husky of her voice. Prester recalled with a shudder how long it had taken him to separate the glamour she'd created for herself in the 'line from how she'd sounded in the bedroom.

Prester pushed aLan's headphone deeper into his ear. "It's for a job—I've got a deadline."

"You can't farm your own?"

"No."

Taylor paused. "This isn't about the New Levites, is it?"

Prester didn't say anything.

"Didn't I tell you not to take that job?"

"Yeah."

"And you took it."

"Yeah."

"Well, fuck you then, Prester." He could hear the cigarette smoke in her voice—he was still quit, ever since they decided to do it together that Christmas.

He decided to hold his tongue, decided not to tell her that not every charmer could still pull college-money from dad. With a record like his, he had few options. He hadn't held an identity long enough in the past two years to put any real-world equity into it, so the best job he had found had been cleaning toilets for the scensters at *Idio*.

Prester steadied his voice. "Taylor, please. Let's just do this—just business."

"Fine," she snapped—he could tell she wasn't doing business, not the kind he wanted. "I'll get you the charms, but I'm going to have to pull them from what's available."

He could tell where this was going.

"Short notice leaves you without many options, Prester—it's gonna take a theft to get what you want."

Damn. He'd only just gotten used to this identity.

"Andrick," he realized.

"Yep," Taylor snapped, exhaling. Her smoke seemed to send static crackles through the 'line. "And he's got clients itching for a hit on their South African."

Prester held his tongue. He thought everyone had abandoned the South African—no one believed in benevolent bankers looking to give away money anymore. At least, so he'd thought.

"All right," he conceded. aLan's task bar paced across the computer screen, looking rather judgmental, Prester thought. "Forward it along, and I'll respond."

"The money's got to be legit," she warned.

"It is—there's just not much of it."

She paused again. "You want this, you deal with the headache. No reports. Nothing."

Prester ran a hand through his hair. It was too oily, he realized. How long had it been since he'd showered?

"I'll play to the scam," he promised. "Just send it along and Pipe the charms to aLan, all right?"

"Have you got a new face ready?" she asked.

He nodded. "Been doctoring it for a few months—figured something would come up sooner or later."

"New security number, birth—credit rec—"

"It's covered, Taylor," Prester interrupted. "I'll give your South Africans a week's worth of transfers and then tank the old face."

"You're going to regret this, Prester."

"I know."

—⁓—

"They're aligned," aLan reported.

Prester stirred awake. Dumbed by fatigue, he took a pull from the mug on his desk, forgetting the effects of naps on coffee. He swallowed with a grimace. aLan had aligned Taylor's charms into the new rite and was slipping the results through the aged plastic lips of Prester's printer. He thought it looked like the machine was gumming the page—a pair of waxy, chapped jaws, trying the alignment out, hoping, perhaps, it was edible. No doubt the printer was as hungry as everything else in Prester's apartment, including himself.

He sat up, groaning with the chair, and started re-arranging his yarn. Taylor had been good for it—aLan's printout had forwards on it that Prester hadn't seen yet, each one promising a different route to the same miracles, the same desires that suckered the charms into life in the first place. Ten friends, ten minutes, three wishes in an hour. Dumb as it had once sounded to Prester, there were enough people who'd try —just in case—and ship the idea along to their friends, families. Things had been different when charmers had relied only on chain letters, but the principle had been the same. Internet had only sped things up. The Pipeline made them insane.

Prester pulled scraps of paper from the piles of envelopes and petitions on his desk. After a few minutes, he'd scribbled out the names of the new charms and pinned them to the wall. He was almost out of yarn, but he had enough to track the new charms' roles in the rite. Different threads for different wishes—ribbons on these, sketches on those, braids for counter-charms. Once aLan got the rite moving, Prester'd sell the wall again. He hoped the Arts Council was still into gutter collage.

"Right," Prester said, stepping away. "Open the reserve charms."

"To whom?" aLan asked mechanically.

"Doesn't matter," Prester told it. "I'm not looking for fireworks here, just a coincidence."

"Set?" he asked after a moment.

"Ready," aLan reported.

Prester closed his eyes. He only needed a few gallons—a minor wish, as it went. He tried to keep Taylor out of his thoughts, tried to keep everything she had and he didn't from souring the charm. It didn't matter; he could feel his resentment staining the small rite. Taylor never had to worry about how many gallons she had in the tank—her father had been buying her metro passes as long as Prester could remember. Had been forking over credits for new clothes, a better pad. New furniture. Prester hadn't held a pass in weeks, and there was no telling how much longer he could keep the Bel Air running. He couldn't even remember what new things smelled like.

"Send 'em," he ordered.

Outside, he smiled. The pad was warm in his pocket—heated by aLan's now-smug computing. Prester had seen the truck parked next to his car in the lot before, but it was always much further down, closer to the pool—nowhere near Prester's dolorous efficiency.

He thumbed open the truck's battered tank-flap and traced a finger over the gas cap. The paint wasn't rusted in here, and the sun hadn't gotten to the cap's dark plastic. He unscrewed it, slipped in his hose and started sucking. A few moments later, the truck bled its noxious fuel down the line. Prester only took a few gallons—he didn't want to push the charms. Having only sent ten to effect the coincidence, he feared things would go bad quickly if he tried to take more than he'd earned.

Afterward, he slid the hose into his trunk and coaxed his old car to life. He'd hoped to get moving earlier, when the sunlight meant the dim, left headlight wouldn't make any difference. Now, he just hoped that the night would slip itself over the car, shrouding as best it could the old thing's derelict complexion. He didn't want to attract attention.

Downtown rolled past his windows in phantasmal lumps, its many signs and streetlights casting multicolored gazes across Prester's windshield. Every building stared at nothing, it seemed, each doing its neon best to be looked at in return but self-blind to know if it was working. Artificial barge-boards clung lamely to the rooflines, their finer details brightened by gap-toothed Christmas lights like lines of glowing birds. People slipped in and out of clubs below, smoking at each other, wandering with the traffic, looking their pointless best and going hurriedly nowhere. Compelled. Saturday was the excuse they gave themselves, but Prester knew there were charmers behind the crowds—there were good reasons why the corner mart's business went dead when it did, why Ladies' Night worked better here than there. Someone wanted a hold-up—another needed a club full of pockets to pick. Charmers made their own opportunities, and different places, different circumstances, decayed as ordered.

When he cleared the avenue and maneuvered through the tree-line, he could only see the city in its paranoid glare atop the mist-slicked boughs of the spruce trees—those that had grown high enough to stare back. Gated communities lifted their parental, wrought-iron fingers as Prester passed—there'd be no decay behind their gates, they promised. Stucco and sheetrock and windows with fake casements—these places had the medical teams that downtown didn't, effecting with their trowels and nail guns the cosmetic surgery that didn't need neon, that didn't blind itself—it only layered scars, and no one here looked for those.

At length, he passed the furthest-adventuring suburbs and moved down the old logging road toward the Levites' estate. Their gate was open when he arrived, and the motion of the moonlight across the shadowed drive looked like an inhalation. Prester looked up at dozens of pairs of laced-together shoes dangling from the Levites' wind-swinging Pipeline cable. He wondered what the old weirdoes thought they had accomplished.

Prester stretched his feet, reclining as best he could across the chair's tucked and pleated leather. The parlor had the same alternately black and white floor tiles that he saw in all these enclaves. He wanted to roll his eyes, wanted to carve something pithy into the yantras and mandalas and god-damned horseshoes tacked above the dark wainscoting.

But he didn't. aLan worked sedulously on a mahogany lowboy at his elbow, porting Prester's rite into the Levites' aged terminal.

"This looks fine, young man," the Levite said. Prester didn't know his name, didn't think they had names.

Prester smiled. "I've done my best, sir."

"Our terminal reports that many of these . . . *charms* are new." The old man studied Prester through his spectacles, the light of faux gas lamps dithering across his pate. "That will make the rite more potent, will it not?"

Prester leaned forward. "Yeah. My rite will keep your database secure, and the new charms mean it will learn faster. The more it encounters, the sooner it will mature—the better it will wish." He glanced at aLan—it was almost finished uploading. "I estimate that it will be fully itself within a month."

"Very good," the old man smiled, hunting and pecking at his keyboard. "I'll just see to this transfer then. Your . . . *familiar* should be able to validate the funds shortly."

Prester swallowed, fishing a slip of paper from the lapel of his battered coat. He offered it to the Levite. "Use the account listed here, if you don't mind."

No sense putting his new money in the old account, just in case any of the South Africans were checking.

The old man squinted as he took the paper. "Of course."

Prester took the cigarettes angrily and stormed through the shop's doors. He felt guilty about smoking, but what did it matter? Who would care? Taylor certainly wouldn't, much as he wanted her to.

Back inside his car, he jammed the cigarette lighter into its nest and accelerated out of the lot. aLan sat coolly on the naugahyde beside him, as blue and uninterested as the light slicking the chrome on Prester's dash. He was glad he'd be switching faces in a week—the tickets that damned community-cop had tossed at him would have eaten everything he earned from the Levites . . . and then some. At least now he'd only lose a quarter of it on a more authentic set of new plates. He could use the rest to get the jump on next month's charms. Maybe, for once, people would be calling him.

Down the road, he eased the Bel Air into one of Idio's narrow parking spaces. The lot winked at him in rainbow flashes, the oils in its pavement awakened by the mist and the moonlight. Prester shoved his pad into his pocket and picked up the cigarettes.

Inside the club, he pulled a pile of cheap placards from another pocket and started handing them out. They promoted a fake show—a band he'd come up with last year—and asked their bearers to spread the word through graffiti and Xerox. The show, Prester's placard promised, would make their wildest dreams come true, but only if they'd spread the word.

At the bar, Fidence, the tender, thrust a meaty finger in Prester's face. "Stop handing that shit out, Prester."

Prester didn't want a fight. He shoved the remaining placards back into his pocket. Later, he'd count them again so he could tell aLan how many he'd released.

He spread his hands placatingly. "Just want a beer, Fid."

"Out," Fidence reported sourly.

"You're out?" Prester challenged. "Of beer?"

"Floated the last keg ten minutes ago," Fidence said. "Damned if Bachs didn't run inventory just last Wednesday. We're gonna lose at least a thousand tonight without it."

Prester's shoulders tightened. First the cop, now this. It was absurd. Idio had never run out of beer, and Prester hadn't pissed anyone off recently—not any charmers. Who'd be throwing wishes at him?

Prester looked around uneasily. "Well, all right. I just came to celebrate."

"Go somewhere else, then," Fidence grunted.

Prester left, unnerved. Outside, a rivet fell from one of the gantry-towers spanning the rail line behind the club. One of the metros chimed its way over the tracks on the other side of the avenue, its over-lit riders like stage-painted extras inside. Prester could see a few looking at him as they slid by.

He had to get to Sixx—Taylor was usually there, and he was starting to worry. Maybe Andrick's charms were no good. Maybe he'd white washed some old ones, and Prester's security-rite was trying to harness dead wishes. He flinched. That always meant trouble.

He eased into his car, stunned when he glanced into his mirror to see a gutter-thread scenster standing at the back of the car. The guy looked like he had sheet-metal skin, like his hair was just head-rust and lichen. The kid's eyes shone with the homogenized orange glow of the surrounding city lights.

Prester turned, but the people he could see crossing the lot looked normal—normal for Idio, anyway. Though he looked, he didn't see anyone in his lane.

He lit another cigarette as he picked his way out of the lot, brakes squealing their distaste for the rain.

Sixx wasn't as crowded as Idio. Prester even liked the music better—they played things downtempo here. He could only take so much drum-and-base from Idio.

Taylor was with some corduroy kids in a corner booth. Prester bummed a light from a passing bearded guy and hurried toward the booth.

He'd broken the guy's lighter.

"Hey, Taylor," he said, anxious.

She looked up, the light from her pad throwing venomous green reflections across her glasses.

"Get that one moving tonight," she told the others.

The kids slid out of the booth, clutching their pads. Prester sat.

"Hey yourself," Taylor said, cinching her shoulders. "Get your rite off?"

"Yeah," he said. "Money's good."

"You're a goddamn idiot," she said, the air-filter clicking in the rafters overhead.

He swallowed. "Yeah? Why?"

"Just wouldn't listen to me, would you?"

He'd play along—decided he *had* to play along. "About what?"

She leaned across a cluster of empty beer glasses. "You've been took."

"By the Levites?" He tried to keep his eyes out of the abyss of Taylor's plunging neckline.

"Designed a security-rite for them, didn't you?" she pressed.

"Yeah."

"They already had one."

"No they didn't," Prester scoffed. "aLan marked their entire grid before I even started collecting charms."

"Yes," she said, "they did. I tried to warn you off, but what the hell do you think I can say over the 'line? Christ, they've got familiars listening everywhere."

He swallowed. Maybe they had other servers, remote units that didn't need to splice from the Pipeline that the main grid used. He shook his head. Even so, aLan would have picked up their relays. No familiar can remain quiet for that long.

She grabbed his hand. "Maybe if you ever came out instead of just calling me when you need favors, I could have given you the jump." She lit a cigarette. "Now you're just fucked."

"Let's say you're right." He palmed the sweat from his brow. "Me laying a new rite over an existing one doesn't mean anything. Nothing wrong with redundancy."

"Except," she said, exhaling rooftops of smoke, "you're the test. You've set yourself up to be screwed and screwed and screwed. You laid out the code, got their terminals loaded with your rite, and then empowered it with your own charms. Fine. Except now, as the charms' suckers forward and sign and mail to their wishing-hearts' content, they're keeping your rite alive, meaning the old one will keep feeding off it."

She took a drag from her cigarette. "Eventually, it'll track the charms back to their source and decide that you're a better target. Hell, it may have figured that out already."

Prester rubbed his face. "Wait."

She folded her arms across her chest.

"Who coded it?" he asked.

"I did. Two months ago."

He scooted closer. "Well, Christ, Taylor—call it off!"

She lidded her gaze. "You think I've got ties to it? Don't be a dumb ass. I took precautions."

Prester could feel the tiny fans in his pad powering up, venting the machine's mechanical heat. "How, then?"

"Damn you," she said, scooting out of the booth. "Come on."

⸺⸺

"No," he protested, pulling away, "let's take my car."

Taylor reached out and grabbed his hand again. "You're lucky you made it this far in it," she hissed. "If you want my help, you're coming with me. By now, the brake fluid's gone, the plugs are corroded—who knows?"

Prester relented and walked with her toward the metro depot. He thought about the cop outside of town. About Idio. Taylor's rite had figured him out—he knew it had.

"I can't believe I'm helping you," she muttered. The mist had congealed into rain, and it was now gathering in shimmering beads on her mostly bare shoulders. "This is stupid."

Prester held his tongue.

On the sidewalk, they picked their way brusquely through the opposing crowd. Everywhere he looked, Prester saw people slicked by the rain, their wet skin and clothes reflecting the city back at him. Neon curves and brickwork smears gathered in the dampened shadows of the walker's dark faces. He saw the walk-sign white men pacing *through* people, stop signs in flashes across wet cheeks. Power lines and metro cables tangled in hair.

One walker slammed into him, his many-ringed fingers crunching against the pad in Prester's pocket—he hoped the stranger hadn't scrambled aLan.

Dragging him onward, Taylor pulled him through a trio of night-outers: long-haired girls in clean sweaters from the campus down the lane. They glared at him with eyes like street signs.

He couldn't be sure if he lost his balance or if a nearby light pole had taken a swipe at him.

When they passed the entrance to the depot, Prester tugged. "The metro?"

She jerked back, flashing a look of wet annoyance at him. "We're walking."

"Where to?" he asked weakly. One of his fake placards flopped from the crowd into a puddle at his feet. Absently, he slid a hand over the pocket where he'd stashed them, but he suspected that this one had come back to him from elsewhere.

Taylor dragged him without answer, slamming him into person after person, banging his shins against smooth-bricked, sidewalk flower gardens. As the traffic thinned, and the buildings stared less at the people and more at each other, Prester started to relax. Here they had shadows, corners and abutments and alcoves without neon, without windows. Places where facades had long since succumbed to the stains of old coal smoke and weak mortar. Prester imagined that these, in the great municipal decay, were only architecturally aware of *themselves*. Aware that, at some other point, there'd been others. A time when they, the buildings, had directed the realities in town. When the integrity of their girders and the strength of their re-bar had dictated at what pace things would change. Now, they knew only that entropy was coming at them from different angles. That things fell apart when they shouldn't, that styles matured and moved on before their time. That, ultimately, they would only be roads.

Prester looked up, watching the rain cascade from a length of the Pipeline between the gutters of two buildings. Its insulation had been agitated bare by the data stream, he could tell—and when he planted his palm against a pock-marked ashlar to brace for Taylor's sharp turn into the alley, he could feel the 'line humming through the stone, animating the self-blind building beyond its time, into tasks it couldn't contain.

He heard things walking behind him as they cleared the alley. Looking over his shoulder, he saw diamond-plate elbows and dumpster-green eyeballs sucked out of his view by the fall of new shadows. They looked now like their metaphors: trash bins and fire escapes. The dark places were groaning in the rain. Taylor's rite was piecing its agents together piecemeal from the city's dying body parts.

Taylor wheeled about—they were standing now in a bricked lane. Coffee shops and book stores lined the far side of the pedestrian mall, and oak trees stretched in stylized planters, their leafy fingers foaming with green-wet light under the glare of nearby security lamps.

"Check the air," she ordered.

Obediently, Prester fished out his pad. Its face had cracked in the collision with the ringed walker, but it had life enough to glow aLan's thoughts. Prester hammered a few quick commands into the pad's rubber buttons, but aLan couldn't detect the Pipeline's wireless gaze here.

"Atmospherics," he reported, looking up. Taylor was tapping at her own pad.

"Let's hope so," she said, her hair now flat against her neck, dark ribbons tracing the bluish veins just beneath her pale skin. Prester's own hair was guiding rain in cold runnels down his back.

"So what now?" he asked, squinting.

Taylor cinched up her shoulders. "By now, your accounts have been reabsorbed—your new faces are gone. I expect your apartment might already have burned down, but the rain may have delayed that."

"Christ," Prester said.

She looked at him. "My rite is bouncing forwards and routing letters by the dozens every minute. It's got chat bots spreading ideas in rooms all across the 'line. It's not that hard for it to get people's wishes aligned," she said. "It just has to encourage the right ones in the right order. I mean," she paused, "none of the wishers knows they're helping it get you when they wish for a shift in road maintenance or a clearing-out of the tenements on your side of town."

"Coincidences," he realized.

"Results, rhetoric," she continued, waving a hand. "The rite can *encourage* them to wish what it wants. Vague is good when you're talking about thousands to harness. The rite only has to harvest 'em up and send 'em where it needs."

Prester laughed. "You mean at me."

"Well, your work, really."

He looked at her. "So why are we here?"

She pointed. Prester followed her arm. They had approached it from a different route, so he didn't recognize the place, but he could see it now. The Arts Council, smug and clean at the end of the mall.

"The collages," he concluded aloud.

She nodded. "Bait and switch."

Prester started dragging *her* this time. If the place was still open, and if he could find some 'line for aLan, they might be able to reuse some of Prester's old rites. Their effects had long since died off, and he could only remember a few of them: job opportunities, a nice table downtown—a carburetor with a longer life. If he could salvage even a few of the charms out of the old yarn-and-newspaper rite-maps, he could set Taylor's rite on a dead trail, send it chasing work down causal lines that no longer existed. Like the buildings around him, Prester would decay himself out of the rite's starving reach. He would reduce himself to dead art: a collection of strings and paper that had long since lost its meaning. A road that went nowhere.

"You're thinking," she said.

"My new face is my old one," he said back, feeling everywhere upon him the harmonics of the rain. The sidewalk hummed beneath its aquatic massage, the gutters sang—the old buildings could hope once again that the sky might wash away some of their entropic scabs. Things were breathing while decay stared at itself with unblinking neon eyes.

He would kick his way into the Arts Council if he had to, if Taylor didn't have any charms that she could work on a forgetful night watchmen and the rotation of the lock. And once inside, he would replace the chain in one of the place's brushed steel commodes with his aged length from Idio. He would let visitors and custodians flush his old chain's power into the walls, back into the art. It would buy the ruse some time.

"Come on," he said, pulling her to him under a nearby awning. He held his breath, hoping that the cigarettes in his pocket would still light.

Taylor laughed, playing along, and thumbed the cigarettes afire with her lighter. They smoked, safe for now, exhaling together into the rain. Giving it back what it was giving them.

The
Dust
and
the
Red

I WAS TEN THE FIRST TIME I SAW THE PEARL. THE SOIL HAD COME loose in Sweetgrass, and to protect the family, my father dug the pearl out of its niche beneath the jamb. He had to clean it, and, since we only had one room, he had no choice but to show us. Taking it outside would have defeated the purpose. Where the dust lived. Where the problems were.

The plains were fast upon us, though I didn't know it then. Only father knew. That's why he extracted the pearl from its rusted tobacco tin. By protecting it, he was protecting us.

He buffed it slowly, evenly, so it would hold mother's paraffin against the dust.

There was no other way.

Jonah was fourteen, and he watched our father. He watched the pearl.

Father looked at me. "Come closer, Caroline," he said.

The tax man was sweating beneath his layers. He wore so many, in blacks: vests, jackets, a hat with curled rims. The landowners came in blacks, and so did the preacher and the lawyers. Black was an invasion. An outfit of shadows for coming inside. Black car, black book, black ink in the pen. Jonah and I stood against the wall, watching mother watching father. I didn't know then that we had the pearl. Jonah had fire in his eyes. He was staring at father, staring at the tax man.

The two men sat very still at our small table. The smell of the morning's pork hung in the air. The stove hadn't quite heated mother's washing water.

"It's the stock exchange," the tax man said.

Father nodded slowly.

"Too many sales," the tax man said. "Nothing left to trade." The tax man bit off the ends of his words as he spoke. Saving bits for later, maybe. Between him and my father, they tried to disturb the air as little as possible.

The tax man glanced again at his black book. Father's fingers were resting on its spine where the tax man had settled it in front of him. It was still closed.

Father nodded again.

"Sign the ledger," the tax man said. "Might not matter. Country's gone broke." He looked out the window.

"Loosened the dust," father said, "out on the plains."

"Most like," the tax man said. "Nothing left of the war-cropping to keep that soil down. Too much, too fast. No time for rotation."

Father nodded. His blond beard glistened where the light found it, oiled by sweat and sunshine. He'd been at the fields when the tax man came—when mother sent Jonah out to collect him, and the tax man stood and sweated outside our front door.

Father's beard looked like the wheat, nodding its secret conversations with the wind and the soil. Nodding that it knew something. Father knew something. He knew what was coming.

"Might need another war, then," he said. "Another demand."

"Might so."

Father signed the tax man's ledger. He licked the pen just like it was a pencil and scribbled his name into the black book.

Jonah stared, with fire in his eyes.

Mother sighed, her hands twisted in her apron.

Outside, the wheat exhaled, stirring the first breeze.

———

Henry's family didn't have a pearl. They didn't come from the same Old Country as the first Lindsay had. They had a little wax man.

It was harvest time then. Henry wasn't working with his father and brothers because of the dust fever. He'd caught it in the summer and, for weeks, coughed and drooled and vomited dirt. He caught it in the devils. He and I and Jonah and the other young Finchers would jump into them. Make games out of who got tossed farthest. I usually won, jerked out of breath—ten, twelve, sometimes fifteen feet. Jonah said it was because I was light. Because I was a girl. The wind was different with girls, he said. It wasn't mad at them.

Henry's skin had changed with the fever. No longer wheat-gold, he was as pale as the new cotton. Henry's family had switched the crops last season, before the soil came loose. Henry looked just like the little wax man, pale and sweating in his father's tiny cellar.

Henry was getting better. He was lucky. There weren't many of mine and Henry's classmates left. A few had survived the fever, the wheat-to-cotton maelstrom that angered the soil. When the new rigs settled, without any fallow rest, the dirt had nested in us—in the lungs and bellies of all of the children. Switching kids—wheat-to-cotton. Wheat-to-cotton. Those as passed on, they went underground to sleep in puddles of fairy mud, mother said, to live in dirt mounds and dark wells. Mother had stories.

Henry said the rigs were the mounds. That their classmates played underground now. He was sore that the fever hadn't taken him down.

"It's all of us," Henry said. "The little man is Fincher himself."

I looked at the little wax man. He had skin like soil rigs—mounded and uneven, pressed into form by fingers, nails, anything that could push. I could see through him a bit, lying there in Henry's palm. Top skin was white and sweating, like Henry Fincher. Inside, he was yellow—old and golden. He was like the Finchers' fields.

"What's he for?" I asked.

"For farming," Henry said. "What every Fincher is for."

"But why do you have him?"

I wouldn't touch Fincher—it looked *warm* in Henry's palm. Mother said to stay away from boys who looked warm. Fincher was close enough to a boy. Molly Haver disappeared last winter—mother said she got too close to somebody too warm. Some boys, most like.

"They wouldn't be no other Finchers without the first one," Henry said. "Father says the cotton'll fix him. Make him all white and proper. When he's all white and proper, we'll be all right. We won't have to go nowhere. Father won't have to sign any more books."

"Don't you have a Lindsay in the cellar, Caroline?" he asked.

"No."

I looked at him, looking for the fire that burned Jonah's eyes when he talked about the pearl.

"We have a pearl," I said. "We're a pearl."

Henry looked confused. "How're you a pearl? You're all Lindsays."

"It's from the Old Country," I said.

Henry curled his fingers around Fincher. With a squint, he pulled it to his lips and blew the dust from its belly.

The little man was made of wax. Must be the Finchers'd be safe, too. Must be the same as the paraffin father smoothed onto the pearl.

Henry blew again, harder. Outside, there was yelling. There was wind. There was dirt between the cotton, as loose as the exchange, father had been saying. Jonah had been saying it, too. The exchange had collapsed, mother told me, so there was nothing to keep the soil in place, to keep them farming. There was nothing to keep their land theirs.

Even the cotton couldn't do it. Outside, Finchers ran between the rigs, heading for the barn, for the corral, for everything that needed to be waxed against the flying dirt. Even the cotton couldn't keep it down.

Henry kissed me then—my first one. A quick, dirty kiss on my cheek. My skin felt warm where he'd pressed his lips.

"Supposed to," he said. "Boys kiss girls."

He coughed.

I nodded. He was holding Fincher tightly. Outside, the sky had become dark.

Our house rolled—end over end over end. End over end. Even so, it didn't go anywhere. We rolled and rolled, stuck in place, everything slipping and falling and gathering in corners. Mother kept at her washing, occasionally grabbing shirts and underwear as they fluttered over her head. The water lapped and wobbled in the basin, but it didn't drip free.

I was laid up in my pallet—a morning of dust fever, but nothing serious, mother said. I was allowed to stay home. Father and Jonah had finished most of the harvest with the other men.

Eventually, the rolling stopped with a crash. Thunder pealed outside, and the windows were dark with wind and dust. It had gathered like red snow upon the blistered panes. There were pots and horseshoes and sacks of flour everywhere. The house hadn't broken, but mother's ladles were still humming from the crash, singing themselves steadily back to quiet.

"Mother," I said, dizzy. Ill. There had been red between my legs that morning. Mother didn't tell father.

There was red again. The rolling and crashing and ringing had stopped. When mother came to put her hands on my shoulders, it was the whole house doing so. The house was dark, and earthy, and tumbled round. There were no corners now.

She gave me some clean cotton, from Henry's grandmother. She had a loom, and her wicker-work fingers tugged at it all day. She never said anything, but she sang mumble-songs like a quiet day in church. She gave us cotton. Mother gave me cotton.

"Do you feel warm?" mother asked.

"No."

"Mother?"

"Yes?"

"What was that rolling?"

Mother's brows came together, gently. Their lines of packed dust like rivers squirming. They came together like fingers, like the hands on my shoulders, like the now-round house, or mother cupping dough. Over and over, cupping and pulling. Coming together again and again.

The house creaked, groaning into the rising wind. Mother looked at the door. Father opened it slowly, his fist clamped onto the back of Jonah's collar.

Mother moved in front of me.

Father's brows came together. In his other hand, he showed mother the pearl.

Mother sighed.

Jonah looked at me. That same fire burning. Curls of dirt rose like smoke upon the wind behind him.

Father looked at us, and without a word, closed the door.

There was red again. It was on my hands, slipping in lines down my back, gathering with the dirt in the soft creases in the backs of my knees. My back felt like fire, and I thought of Jonah.

Henry had dropped the melon when the shot cracked across the farm. He kept running.

I lay between the rigs, unable to move. I didn't cry. It was getting dark, and Mr. Bradford wouldn't find me if I didn't cry. My back was burning from the shot. From Mr. Bradford's shotgun. I lay still and let the red gather. I let it shhh the soil. The melon vines were quiet in their unstable dirt where I lay.

When Mr. Bradford found me, he didn't look angry. He saw where Henry had dropped the melon between the rigs. It was smooth and white and red with the wet of the setting sun. He pulled me up gently and pressed a shotgun shell into my fist.

"Take that to your father," Mr. Bradford said.

"Yes, sir."

"You tell him it was dark."

"Yes, sir."

"Who was that with you?"

I thought about the little wax man. Henry said there wasn't any yellow any more—it was all white and proper. Fincher was all white and proper.

Father's fields were turning brown with the dusts. Two acres had already browned up and disappeared, slipping between the rigs, consumed by their own fevers. Underground in the fairy mud now. He had signed another book last week.

It had been Mr. Fincher's book. A new, black book with white, white pages.

"You won't say," Mr. Bradford said.

Between my fingers, I balled sticky blood into the quiet soil, rolling and rolling it. Smooth and round. A bloody, dirty me. I wouldn't say. I dropped the little me and pushed it into the rig with my foot.

I didn't come out of the ground until I was back home.

Inside, father took the shotgun shell wordlessly. Mother watched, her fingers coming together at her sides when she saw the red down my back.

Father peeled back the shell's wax and split its little, wedged mouth right open. He turned the shell over, and rock salt piled into his palm.

He gave the salt to mother, who wrapped it in cheesecloth and set it on her counter.

"You were with Henry Fincher?" he asked me, his brows parting.

I wouldn't say. I hadn't seen Fincher in two years. I hadn't seen how white he'd become. Henry was just Henry. Henry Fincher was a waxen boy who could turn the fields white and proper. His brothers could turn the fields white and proper. His sisters were always white now, pale and snowy. Their mother had hired workers of her own to pick the white fields. She and the Fincher girls stayed as white as could be. Whiter than the pearl, even.

Father's fields didn't turn at all.

He extracted the pearl from its tin under the jamb. For a time, he shifted his stares between me and the pearl. He had shaved his golden beard, and the lines in his jaw were like the rigs themselves.

"I'm going to see Fincher," he said, clutching the pearl. He stared hard at me.

"Will he mind Jonah's place?" mother asked.

"I'll see that he does," father said.

He didn't look at me as he closed the door.

———

When mother had done with me, when we'd done with Grandmother Fincher's cotton, we joined father and Jonah outside. The winds had quieted; the fields were quiet in their rows and rows. A cluster of Jonah's friends were watching us from far away. They looked like tiny stick men, standing so far and so still.

Father still had Jonah by the collar. When Jonah looked at me, the fire had grown brighter in his eyes.

Father extended a handful of marbles to mother. They shone in all colors, in cloudy and painted glass, chipped and smooth, like the inside of the house. Rounded by rolling and rolling and rolling.

I looked at the stick-boys. Jonah had never owned a marble.

Mother took them.

"He won them," father said.

Jonah's fingers came together at his sides. Fists.

"How?"

"With the pearl. He was shooting with the pearl."

With the house. With us.

Rolling and rolling.

All of us rolling, bouncing against other tiny worlds, other dusty, waxen places with other dusty problems. With other things coming together.

"Give them back," mother said. "You played unfair."

Jonah said "No."

Father extracted the pearl from his pocket. The air felt clean as it brushed against our freed skin. "This is a family, Jonah."

"And look what it did, father," Jonah said. "Look what I can do with the whole family."

Father looked at him. Mother began walking toward the stick-boys.

I watched father drag Jonah to mother's vegetable garden. I watched him stand him up on the scarecrow's mount. I watched him tie his arms and legs against the ragged hickory beams. Father couldn't punish him with more work. Work was the family. Work was the pearl, and Jonah would work with the pearl. He wanted to work with the pearl. His eyes burned when he looked at the pearl, watching it doing nothing. Waxy and sweating in its tiny, dark places. Waiting just to roll and shine and lord in the sun. Like mother's stories. The fairy kings under the water. The pearls they traded in Inverness, the ones they stole on the Prince of Wales—the boat from the Old Country. The tobacco tins they collected in Carolina. That Lindsay himself worked for before coming first to Kansas, then to Texas, then everywhere else. They'd kicked him off the high land, mother said, in the Old Country.

Father could only punish Jonah by giving him to the rows for a bit. Just a bit.

He would only leave him up there for a bit, father would later say.

"You'll go to Boston," mother said. "You and Henry, after the wedding."

"Where's Boston?" I asked.

Mother sat still at the table. "It's near the water. A bit closer to the Old Country."

"Were you ever there?"

"No."

"Who will help you around here?" I asked.

"Mother won't need help," father said, his jaws coming together. "We're leaving."

He had the pearl-tin clutched tight in his fist. He hadn't given it to Fincher. When he went that night.

"We'll pick fruit in the sun," mother said. "In California. I won't need help."

"Where's California?" I asked.

"That doesn't matter."

I started crying then. The house came together. After so long. After so long since the rolling and rounding and crashing together. After so much time soft and dark and earthy, its corners came back together. Already, it looked emptier.

"What about Jonah's grave?"

After so long since Jonah.

"Fincher won't till there," father said. "Gave his word."

Father came back that night with the pearl. He paid his last debt to Fincher with our land. He couldn't give up the pearl—it was all of us. Even Jonah.

In Boston, Henry would be going to a school. Fincher had grown so white, had begun to glow in his cellar, that the family was sending itself in all directions. The girls would go to

Savannah. Henry and his brothers would learn New England business. The house would be used for the new workers staying behind. The ones with no money. The ones who had long since signed everything away with dark ink in dark ledgers. And what they had signed away had never come back together.

Father paid my way. He couldn't release the pearl. He couldn't close the debt without the land.

Without me.

There was red in the sky when I looked out the window. Mother's skin reflected the red light, but father's eyes were gathering its shadows. It had gotten into him, the red.

The plains were nigh upon us, and they were red, red, red.

Mother gave back the marbles. Jonah had only been on the hickory a little while. We were sitting at the table when the red, red clouds stole the sky. The house snapped and creaked and threw things. It blew heavy dust at us from beneath the windows, through the doorjamb, and from the small, puckered mouths in the clinker-built siding. Everything was dust and the screaming, red sky.

Father jerked open the door, and the dust came in. It attacked him. Straight from the loosened rigs, flying like so many bullwhips. Flakes of whitewashed siding, ripped from the house and pulled by the eddy inside, painted the new bloodspots on father's skin. They filled the little wounds, white and proper. When he got up again, he screamed Jonah's name and fought the wind, but the dust pushed him back down. The house was a cave now.

Mother shut the door from behind. She touched father's head where it leaned against the wall. She stared out the window, as the storm screamed back at father.

The red sky turned black. The house rolled and rolled. And this time, it did not stay in place. I found the tobacco tin beneath the doorjamb, and I clutched it against my chest. Inside, the pearl rolled and rolled in circles against the edges, clanging and screaming against the metal as it went. I held it tight and rolled and rolled.

The fire died with Jonah. Now there's nothing to burn away the dark. The fields, white and proper, are as tar-black as the sky. The Finchers, scattered, are everywhere as morose as my Henry—I read as much in their letters. Troubled and displaced. I have learned.

Fincher, somewhere, must be sealed against the dusty night which is now ever-present upon the plain, in the Bowl, they call it. Fincher's soft flesh, though it is still right and proper, can no longer breathe. He can no longer be molded within whatever safe canister his wardens have sealed him. He has lost his warmth.

The pearl went with my parents. In the sun, in California, where I imagine them picking orange after orange, coming together at night to watch the sun set over such a large place, coming together to keep the pearl in their palms. There is no wax upon its skin in all that sun, and we are vulnerable again to whatever blows upon us. Though the Bowl has gone dark, and stays so, I need only worry about what falls upon me here.

The clouds of Jonah's great storm have blown so high, they weep upon Boston. Every day, it is red rain that falls, droplets of Old Egypt's Nile, the rain of wrath and fire. My Henry, is, of course, nothing but wax. Static though his Wax Fincher is, nothing can get through the family's richened, white-and-proper flesh.

But I am no longer a Lindsay, I can roll no longer, and I haven't the flesh-of-wax Fincher blood to keep me clean against all the red rain. I have only the name. My children are as imperturbable as their father, and they wear clothes every day in shades of rich black over their cream-white skins.

I have only the red rain. Everywhere there is red, and nothing rolls in this house of many corners. Nothing comes together, not even Dr. Marchant's laudanum-tonics. Not the rest-treatments, not even the salts, thick and rocky as they are—like the shot still burning clean against my spine, still buried in my flesh. I am my mother's salt-filled cheesecloth, and I keep cotton for the blood.

Henry buys me Old Country pearls whenever he can, but they do not hold wax.

I listen to the wind and the rain, and between treatments, I roll. Between treatments, things come together.

Artaud Wells, executor
Estate no. 0102-0125, *de Blainville*
Lot appraisal 3821-06 (affidavit 3821-b)
[SIGNATORY WAIVED]

Artaud:

Attached, please find our bibliographer's analysis for de Blainville Lot 3821-06. Dr. Paulin Gáribe's chemical analysis appears in appendix ii, Dr. Anna Singlest's commentary in appendix iii, and Dr. Anima Nandwani's in appendix v. The accompanying affidavits will appear under separate cover (excepting 3821-b, reproduced here as appendix vi), each from the analysts' respective laboratories and universities. We now record these in triplicate, so sign all three of each and return a copy to us. At the direction of one of our new insurance providers, we've included notarized memoranda in duplicate following the appendices: the documents stipulate that we request (and you agree) to provide a copy of each of the analysts' affidavits for the de Blainville heirs. The other copies are for your records.

Our bibliographer assures us he will return the lot by this weekend. Let the matter of his scanning and uploading the documents be done between us. Following last week's deposition, both your lawyers and ours signed off on the agreement (cf. "Fair Use," appendix vii: Millennial Philology Subscription and accredited partners). It is for posterity and research that our agent made his copy—even if, I grant, he should have first acquired leave. As he told us, he did it without thinking—a scholar's reflex, perhaps. Let me encourage you to acquire a transcript of the deposition, which includes the record of the bibliographer's testimony, for it is both disturbing and brilliant. He felt (and still does) as if the documents scanned and uploaded themselves—as if, through his analytic processes, their perpetuation occurred as a foregone matter of course.

I think he may simply have acted on his bookish instincts without thinking. Regardless, the lot is undamaged, and we regret the inconvenience to the de Blainville heirs.

All best.
—Robert

Encl.: bibliographic analysis, Lot 3821
index of title-page facsimile images
Gáribe: chemical analysis
Singlest: socio-historical analysis
Facsimile manifest, Abergavenny House, 1666
Nandwani: site-specific socio-historical analysis
Electronic-facsimile subscription royalty agreement
Facsimile, affidavit 3821-b

o

Appendix i

Bibliographic Analysis: lot 3821
Estate no. 0102-0125, *de Blainville*
[SIGNATORY, Aubrick & Wain, Inc.]

Disclosure of Electronic Publication: *An Anonymous Salvage* (and accompanying analysis)

For Use by Subscription: Millennial Philology Subscription (and accredited partners)

Per my agreement with Aubrick & Wain, Inc. and the de Blainville Estate, I, the attending bibliographer (lot 3821), have made a full facsimile reproduction of *An Anonymous Salvage* and my accompanying analysis. This digital document will be accessible only by subscription (cf. agreement regarding the de Blainville estate's due-royalties) as approved by Mr. Artaud Wells (appendix vi).

With this analysis, I release my appraisal to Aubrick & Wain, Inc.; a copy exists in undisclosed safety-deposit (per appraisal agreement 3821-06, affidavit 3821-b), should a problem arise. All correspondence regarding the appraisal should be routed through Aubrick & Wain, Inc. or its approved agents.

It is my hope that by publishing lot 3821 in this manner, I have aided its perpetuation in a manner that will facilitate new methods by which this fey document can continue its fey business. Let the analyses of those scholars who follow my interest in lot 3821 be, themselves, the first of these new methods.

Collation Formula:
[paper:] various 2°, 4°, 8°, 16°: π^2, A-C^8, D^8(-D$_7$), ^{x}A^8 [E], ^{x}A^{13} [F], ^{x}A^4 [G], π^2 [$\$_1$ signed] 59 leaves, unnumbered [p.p. 1-118] 190 mm X 140 mm; 20-23 lines; various type, handscript; body & face, various;

Title Page: $\pi_2{}^a$
Crown, 2°: π^2, chain 23-25 mm.; [paper:] large post; [watermark:] horn HRB

HIGHGATE RAG & BONE | *An Anonymous Salvage* | Willord B. Delby, printer & binder | Pennwick Bindry, Pennwick Ln. 1783
[type:] body 86; face 84 X 3: 5

Binding:
Red calfskin over pasteboards, untooled; 193 mm X 143 mm X 10 mm.; no title; grain relief, .75 mm.

Bibliographer's Notes:
The first two leaves of Lot 3821, *An Anonymous Salvage*, (identical in composition and measure to the book's final two) are of a kind with the endpapers, each watermarked with large post's characteristic horn watermark—in turn imposed with HRB for the Highgate Rag & Bone. Dr. Paulin Gáribe concludes in his chemical analysis that "the endpapers, as well as the first and last two leaves in the book, are made from fibers of varying ages, some as many as two hundred years apart. A great many of

the fibers in the paper exhibit signs of having previously carried inks, dyes, or other resins" (*cf.* appendix ii, introduction). This analysis strengthens the seemingly foregone conclusion that the various documents collated into the book were recovered from a rag-and-bone shop, where, most likely, they would have been rendered unto new paper—as was the case with the documents and fabrics that were recycled into the endpapers. However, Anna Singlest, in her socio-historical analysis (appendix iii), finds no record of there ever having existed either a "Highgate Rag & Bone" or a "Pennwick Bindry." For that matter, she can find no record of a Pennwick Lane, either. I see nothing untoward in her findings, as any number of people may have called any number of businesses (and the streets upon which they were located) by any number of different names during the period of the book's collation.

Essentially, Lot 3821 is a collation of documents that perpetuate their own textual (and physical) survival. It is, of course, indeterminable whether the documents were recovered from the shelves of Highgate Rag & Bone by the shop's owner or by some rag-picking client with a keen eye for bibliographic rarity. While, Dr. Singlest tells us, it would not have been unheard of for such rare and mysterious documents to have found their way into such a shop, it still would have been "highly unlikely," as the eighteenth-century fascination with "curiosities" would have, most likely, recovered these materials from various auctions and sales of estate before they ever reached a rag-and-bone. Certainly one or two may have slipped past *curiosity*'s vigilant gaze, but for four to do so, each espousing similarly strange meta-textuality, seems to me a coincidence of the most improbable order. It is more likely that some other, as-yet undetermined agency facilitated the discovery of these documents as a group in what would have been the categorical madness and document-crowding of a rag-and-bone shop's shelves.

My bibliographic analysis of the individual documents collated in Lot 3821, *An Anonymous Salvage*, follows below—the collator's are titles separated from their documents' analyses in each case by a single, broken rule, excepting the dual pamphlets of "The Humours," which I present together.

o

Life

———————————————————————————————

Collation:
pot, vellum 8º: A-C^8, D^8(-D$_7$) [\$$_1$ signed] 30 leaves, unnumbered [p.p. 1-60] 190 mm X 140 mm (B$_1^a$); 20 lines; A-C^8, D$_1^a$-D$_6^b$: French Bastardia; body 122; face 120 X 3: 5

Title Page: A$_1^a$
Le Livre de les personnes malades | *rappelez-vous à vos voisins* | MDLXIV | [image: "Doktor Schnabel von Rom" ("Doctor Beak from Rome") engraving, Rome 1656, 125 mm X 100 mm (cf. facsimile i)] | Life
[last line handwritten: commensurate with type]
(Facsimile i, "Doktor Schnabel von Rom")

Bibliographer's Notes:
This first section of the collection, titled Le Livre de les personnes malades: *rappelez-vous à vos voisins* (The Book of the sick people: *remember to your neighbors*), by its printer (and "Life" by the overall collection's later collator), dates from 1564 CE, as evidenced by the roman numerals on its title page. It is comprised of four octavo gatherings, the last of which is missing its final two leaves, and the title page is printed in unremarkable French Bastardia. The gatherings appear to have been signed by the collator who titled them "Life," the signatures appearing uniformly on the recto of the first leaf of each gathering. Curiously, however, the vellum has been trimmed to the dimensions of early seventeenth-century pot paper. In my opinion, the work had not one editor but several, each of which added some different innovation as the catalogue came to his concern. The vellum itself is poorly made and heavily wormed. I cite here a portion of Dr. Gáribe's chemical analysis (cf. appendix ii, report 1^A):

[T]he calfskin appears to have been inadequately limed prior to being stretched, facilitating, it would seem, varying microbial infestations. Furthermore, the worming patterns in the pages are consistent with those attributed to the common book louse (*Trogium pulsatorium*), suggesting that the colonies provided the proper environments for mold and other decayed matter upon which the book louse feeds. As there is no significant water damage to the vellum, I cannot conclude any other source for these organic anomalies.

The inadequate liming, Dr. Gáribe unofficially posits in his cover letter, may have been a result of shortages of calcium oxide during the period, as most of mainland Europe (as well as the British Isles) had depleted its supplies treating the corpses of the victims of the various plague epidemics from the previous two centuries with quicklime in mass graves. It is impossible to determine precisely what sort of organisms could have survived in the poorly limed vellum, even if only for short periods. The book louse is, however, a better candidate than most.

It appears as if these gatherings are only the first four (excluding the missing final leaves from the fourth gathering) of a larger, no longer extant, number. A_1^b-B_3^b record, in two columns per page, French, Dutch, and Italian names, each apparently signed by its owner—or, perhaps, someone surviving the name-holder. B_4^a-D_3^b record not names but personal marks. It is impossible, of course, to determine if these signatories were merely mimicking what they already saw in the book when it came to them or if more literate community members decoded the pattern for them.

I join Dr. Gáribe in unofficially theorizing that if book lice survived and reproduced within the vellum itself, and if they carried the *Yersinia pestis* enterobacteria, the circulation of the book as a list of plague sufferers to be remembered would almost certainly itself have been a communicator of the Bubonic Plague, of which history records a general European resurgence in the early 1560s. In this sense, the documents would have kept themselves alive by spreading the plague that provided their meaning. Under these fantastic circumstances, the book louse, the *Yersinia pestis*, and the text all shared a common interest in perpetuation—even in the face of the best efforts to the contrary by the people facilitating their survival.

○

The Humours

———

Collation:
pot 8º: ˣA⁸ [$₁ signed, ˣA signed as E by collator] 8 leaves, unnumbered [p.p. 1-16] 190 mm X 140 mm (ˣA₂ᵃ); 23 lines; ˣA⁸: English Cursiva; body 82; face 80 X 2: 3
[paper:] ˣA: chain 24-6 mm.; pot; pot MC

Title Page: ˣA₁ᵃ
A Difcoverie of Curios Humour | AN ALKEMICAL PAMPHLET | in Phlegmatic Ink | [rule 97 mm] | Printed by | The Metallers Companie, George Taylo, William Kenwick. 1627 | for the Worfhipful Companie of Stationers | The Humours | Phlegm
[last two lines handwritten: commensurate with non-italic type]

Bibliographer's Notes:
This second segment of the collection, titled "The Humours: Phlegm" by the collator, fits its printing characteristics better than "Life." The leaves in this gathering were printed from a sheet of pot paper (an at-the-time French rarity in early seventeenth century England) bearing a dexter-facing pot watermark. The "MC" on the mark is, assumedly, an imposition the printers commissioned for their sheets. The paper itself has suffered some degree of decomposition, as evidenced by the sharp .25 mm relief of its chain lines. Unlike the vellum in "Life," however, the leaves in "Phlegm" have not been artificially trimmed to mimic the conventions of another medium—they *are* the other medium of "Life."

It appears that the entirety of the pamphlet is contained within "Phlegm'"s single, 8º gathering. Its contents, printed for the Worshipful Company of Stationers, outline the alchemical philosophy behind (and practical creation of) waterproof ink. The authors (perhaps the printers Taylo and Kenwick themselves) lay out a simple ink recipe derived from hawthorne, the soot left by pine smoke, wine, and common oils; however, their recipe also includes "phlegm," the humour that resists change and is associated with water. The author is not specific with the chemical makeup of "phlegm," but it is clear by the tone of address that he or she is writing to an informed audience.

Dr. Gáribe's second analysis reveals that exposure to water (he theorizes a flood) is to blame for the paper's decomposition (appendix ii: 2^f). However, Dr. Singlest (appendix iii) provides an alternative explanation. In 1625, her report explains, fire engines (crude things quite dissimilar to our contemporary devices) made their first appearances in London. Many seventeenth-century texts were lost not as a result of the fires that occasionally ravaged London; rather, the valiant-yet-damaging efforts of the fire brigade accelerated their decay, as most buildings burned too hot—therefore too quickly, Singlest explains—to cause widespread flashfire upon the texts in these unfortunate buildings. That the fires spread so quickly, Singlest explains, contributes to misconceptions about their durations.

Dr. Gáribe's report reveals that, unlike the paper itself, the ink with which the pamphlet (or "Phlegm") was printed is itself waterproof. Among its dyes and oils, the ink contains chemicals that bonded with the cellulose in the paper's fibers. Much like "Life," "Phlegm," then, facilitates its own survival in the face of the accidentally deleterious enterprises of men. In this case, fire-fighting.

It bears noting that Singlest includes in her report that Abergavenny House (the locus of operations for the Worshipful Company of Stationers) burned down in the great fire of 1666. Among their reported losses, however, texts printed after 1627 numbered surprisingly few (cf. facsimile manifest, appendix iv).

Collation:
arms 16°: $^xA^{13}$ [$\$_1$ signed, ^xA signed as F by collator] 13 leaves, unnumbered [p.p. 1-26]; 190 X 140 mm ($^xA_2{}^a$) 23 lines; $^xA^{13}$: English Cursiva; body 82; face 80 X 2: 3
[paper] ^xA: chain 22-24 mm.; arms; arms of England

Title Page: $^xA_1{}^a$
Embaraffing the Fires | AN MONOGRAPH FOR PRINTERS | *On the charming off the yellow bile for the publifhing of books* | [rule 83 mm] | [image: London During the Great Fire, engraving,

Visscher, 73 X 124 mm. (cf. facsimile ii)] | Enscombe Marque, Esq. and William Wurt, printers | 1674 | The Humours | Yellow Bile

[last two lines handwritten: commensurate with non-italic type]

(facsimile ii, London During the Great Fire, Visscher, engraving)

Bibliographer's Notes:

It is difficult to tell, without disassembling the binding of the overall collation, whether or not "Yellow Bile" and "Phlegm" were first collated as a single brochure before being later sewn into the overall collection. However, since the contents of both concern themselves with two of the four classical humours, I consider the issue highly probable. The contents of "Yellow Bile" (the humour associated with the element of fire) were printed on a sheet of arms paper bearing 22-24 mm chain lines (N.B. these do not exhibit the same characteristics of decay as found in "Phlegm"). The gathering also contains the "arms of England" watermark, which is understood to have first appeared in the printing trade during the year of "Yellow Bile"'s printing: 1674. The engraving that appears (in a double-rule frame) on the title page later appears in Robert Chambers's well-known *Book of Days*, first edition. It is impossible to tell if the image's appearance in Marque's and Wurt's pamphlet inspired Chambers's usage or if the matter is merely coincidence.

The material within "Yellow Bile" concerns itself with the production and use of "fire-embarassing" paper. Marque and Wurt paraphrase "historical documents" (from which they do not quote directly) detailing the drawing of fiber from sheets of glass and then arranging these fibers into flexible sheets that, when woven into at least 30% pulp fiber, can be printed upon. When queried, Dr. Gáribe theorized that, even should all of the pulp combust, the residual ink-content remaining upon the un-burned fiberglass could be sufficient to re-create a document's original text (appendix ii: 3ª). Furthermore, he concludes, it is unlikely that the destruction of all 30% of the pulp-fiber would compromise the integrity of the fiberglass sufficiently to completely destroy the "paper." Since the ink with which "Yellow Bile" was printed matches the ink from "Phlegm" in chemical composition, I am led to conclude that the inclusion of the pulp-fiber in the "paper" was simply to provide the cellulose necessary for the "phlegmatic ink" to achieve its permanency, the fiberglass, of course, lacking this itself. In this regard, Marque's and Wurt's "embarrassing" paper would offer printers' texts protection both from fire and the water used later to douse it. Without an example to consult, I am unable to conclude whether or not only 30% of the text (assuming the other 70% of the inked material as having run from the fiberglass in the event of a dousing) would be sufficient to re-create the text's intended content. It should have been enough, I am convinced, to paraphrase and redact, however, enabling printers to offer, in the worst-case scenario, a close approximation of the documents ruined by a fire brigade's noble efforts.

I find it easy to deduce the reasons behind Marque's and Wurt's anxieties given the proximity of their pamphlet's printing to the great fires that ravaged London in 1666. Singlest replied, when queried, (appendix iii:8b) that the sheer size of the real estate involved in the Great Fire resulted in longer-smoldering flames (fed by the super-heated thermals created by such a confluence of burning architecture) that, theoretically, could have induced flash-fire upon any purely fiber-based documents in close enough proximity.

o

Man

—————————————————————————————————————

Collation:
foolscap, 4⁰: ${}^{x}A^{4}$ [$\$_1$ signed, ${}^{x}A$ signed as G by collator] 4 leaves, unnumbered [p.p. 1-8]; 190 X 140 mm (${}^{x}A_2{}^{a}$) 20 lines; ${}^{x}A^{4}$: Caslon's Roman, leaded / Bengla handscript; body 88; face 86 X 4: 5

[paper] ${}^{x}A$: chain 25-29 mm.; foolscap; no mark

Title Page: ${}^{x}A_1{}^{a}$
PAPER STEWE | কাগজ, পত্রিকা খায়া | [rule 86 mm.] | *A Recipee* | Printed for The Sifters of Our Ladie of Greater Peace |

by Abraham Gould, London 1767 | [rule 85 mm.] [image: "Cover Page of 'The Life of the Virgin Mary,'" woodcut (cropped). Albrecht Dürer, 1511, 85 X 75 mm. Copperplate frame, 102 X 95 mm. (cf. facsimile iii)] | [rule 85 mm.] | *for the relief of Beengal famine*

["Man," handwritten: commensurate with non-italic type]

(facsimile iii, "Cover Page of 'The Life of the Virgin Mary,'" woodcut. Albrecht Dürer, 1511)

Bibliographer's Notes:

This segment of the collection, titled "Paper Stewe" (the accompanying Bengla title transliterates as "Paper Eat," a poor translation according to Anima Nandwani (cf. appendix v)), details a recipe for the cleaning and softening of pulp paper for human consumption, ostensibly (as evidenced by the prioress's prayer printed on $^{x}A_1^{b}$) to relieve the famine that had beset the Bengali region in 1766, where, according to Dr. Nandwani (appendix v: 9^{b}), the priory of the Sisters of Our Lady of Greater Peace was (and still is) located. Perhaps the most salient feature of this pamphlet is its bilingual nature: beginning with $^{x}A_1^{b}$, the verso of each leaf details the "paper stewe" recipe and outlines appropriate prayers of thanksgiving in Caslon's 1728 leaded, Roman type; the recto of each successive leaf offers a translation of the same in handscript Bengla. This leads me to believe that the distribution of the pamphlet would have been limited, given the time involved in the Bengla translation and the limits of the timeframe within which the Sisters would have wanted to get their text into general circulation to be of use to those suffering as a result of the famine.

The text itself appears on unremarkable foolscap 4° leaves. The title page contains the boss of the Sisters of Our Lady of Greater Peace in a period copperplate frame: Dürer's original woodcut cover image for the 1511 printing of "The Life of the Virgin Mary." Dr. Nandwani reports that she was unable to find any extant records detailing either the success or the failure of the Sisters' campaign to alleviate famine by encouraging its sufferers to consume what printed materials they could find. Dr. Gáribe's chemical analysis of this pamphlet (appendix ii: 4^{c}) titled "Man" by the collection's collator, reveals that the ink contains high traces of lead, perhaps communicated by the type itself. In any event, consuming this particular book would have been, to say the least, unpleasant.

In regards to textual content, it bears noting that by being the document (or one of them) that outlines the recipe for the safe consumption of pulp-paper, "Man," ensures its own textual survival at the possible expense of any and all other pulp-paper documents. Should a similar famine strike this or another society in the future, however, "Man"'s inclusion in the overall collection wouldn't necessarily ensure the survival of the other gatherings (indeed, the other materials would become the most readily available ingredients for the rendering of the "stewe").

The Heresy Box

November 12, 1:45 AM—

Gwen held my hand on the train—I couldn't tell why she was smiling beneath the shroud of her thin hair. Ordinarily, I wouldn't take odd routes with strangers, but she was cute, and she knew my name. I suppose I didn't mind the scars on her temples—they seemed to be going around.

She must have had something to do with the hypoderm in my pocket—I didn't ask. There'd be time at the clinic for answers.

The tips of her hair swayed as she leaned into one of the train's parabolic windows.

"Did they give you an extra hypo?" she asked.

I smiled. "Are you feeling—"

"Let me see it," she said, settling cool fingers along my neck.

I fished the injection out of my pocket and settled it in her palm. "Don't you think—"

She tucked it into her cardigan.

"I'll take care of it," she said.

November 12, 1:17 AM—

After I wandered through the Collection Apse and filed my information, I emerged again into the damp evening. A tepid breeze had gathered while I was inside.

Some elbow-patched bum thrust a flyer at me, meeting my gaze only for an instant. I watched him dispense his pages just as mechanically to at least three other people.

I wondered why he had scars on his temples.

The flyer offered a name and an address and a few strategic quotes from Yeats and Byron. The masthead said "Homeopathy" and something about "Stigma 51"—it would be on a ballot next week.

My throat tightened, and I began to sweat. A fragment from last night stabbed through my amnesia. I shut my eyes and tried to force it away. God, I didn't want to go back to the hospital.

It was no use.

I remembered that the dirt had peppered her lips, but it didn't matter—I didn't even know who she was. She had been glowing. It was warm, and nothing made sense. The hospital just didn't have answers.

With a sigh, I realized I needed the memory—I needed last night back. If I could recall how, exactly, I'd violated the Register, I could ensure I never did it again. Recalling the sin would mean secondary infection, no doubt, but it would be better than accidentally incurring another blackout.

The breeze moved on, so I caught my breath and found the nearest train schedule—I would need a different line to get to this clinic, where, no doubt, these homeopaths could tease my memory with stabs and fragments until, at last, it grew tired and filled in its own gaps.

A brunette sidled up beside me. She clutched one of the bum's flyers as the breeze tossed her hair across her face.

"You headed this way?" she asked, pointing at the page.

I took a deep breath—the reverend-doctors had sent me with a spare injection, after all.

"Sure," I said, "why not?"

She took my hand. "I'm Gwen."

"Mark."

"I know."

November 12, 12:20 AM—

A glowing square chased the sins out of my head. Phantasmal simulations of larceny and insecticide thrashed in piecemeal chunks along my conscious periphery, repelled, it seemed, by the square. Text effervesced upon it like hazy cuneiform. With one dying stab at the light, a violent memory rallied and surged. I think the enceph simulated me through a murder. I couldn't tell —they did strange things with adrenals.

Sweat had effloresced everywhere upon my body, and I was breathing in desperate gasps—my clothes had been replaced with a gown. Meanwhile, a number of other squares had joined the first, and they now filled the wall at my feet. I thought they had shifted from ancient sticks and wedges to something younger, something more clear—Aramaic, perhaps? Koine?

When my eyes stopped throbbing, I realized that it was English: the squares had been switched on, I suppose, to show me who was now doing what. They were diplomas—fifteen of them— that must have been downloaded to the chamber while I was out. As I waited for my nausea to pass, I read them: certificates of ordination at Hindu, Unitarian, and new-Cath seminaries— graduate degrees and residencies. Insignia of hospitals from all over the Northeast shone like tiny ornaments at the bottom of each screen.

"Glad to have you back," the intercom said.

"Yeah," I said, turning my head. I could see steel wainscoting and enameled colonettes. No one else was in the chamber, but I could hear actuators wiggling behind the little saints on the frescoed walls—they looked cyanotic in the dim light.

"I haven't seen such a reaction in some time," another voice said through the intercom. "Anaphalaxis is rare."

I nodded dumbly. "You took care of it?"

"We did," a third said.

"So," I licked my lips, "what have I got?"

The reverend-doctors paused.

"There were anomalies in your Douay-enceph," the first finally said, "so we also tested your levels against both the Vedic and Rheims codices."

"And?"

"Do you remember how you spent your evening yesterday?" asked the second.

I squinted. There had been a party, something outdoors. I remembered a bonfire—some people had taken off their clothes.

"Am I allergic to nudity?" I asked.

"No," the second said. It amused me a little that they spoke in turns. "Do you recall anything else?"

I struggled. There had been people with antlers—I think I had sex in a field. I remembered that we had thrown just about everything we could find into the fire. How had I gotten there, though? What had we been chanting?

"Well," I said, clearing my throat, "A fire, naked people. I remember being happy."

They paused again.

"We believe you were at a sabbat," the first said. "Our reports are conclusive—you are dangerously allergic to them."

I began to sweat again—even the suggestion didn't agree with me.

"Our guess," reverend-doctor two said, "is that you would experience similar symptoms in the presence of any form of the occult."

"I theorize," number three said, "that had you actually known what you were participating in, you would have suffered more than hives and fever—a coma, most likely."

The diploma-screens began to darken.

"An acolyte will arrive shortly with your prescription," number two said. "You'll need to return for inoculations every three months."

"We'll also provide you with a sanctuary-table," number three added. "Regular, notarized attendance at any state-subsidized facility will reduce your co-pay."

The screens darkened entirely—fluorescent light now slithered down the chamber's walls.

I waited, but the voices didn't say anything else, so I passed a few minutes alone on the freezing catafalque before an orange-draped acolyte shuffled in. He administered the injection and reviewed the sanctuary-table with me—I'd been to a few of its registries before but only to take care of my yearlies. He promised that the inoculation would wipe the diagnosis within an hour. I, like many, couldn't be trusted with my own memories— in some cases, they caused relapse.

Afterward, he delivered a short lecture praising the Epistemic Register. I'd heard this number before: mandate this, subsidy that. Health care.

⁓

November 11, 7:03 PM—

The triage nun held my wrist delicately, her thin nails aligned with the lines of my palm. The vial at my elbow didn't need support—it depended from a filament in the confessional's screen. My blood looked almost silver as it slicked the glass.

"My father had allergies," I said. I knew at least that about him.

I could hear garbled summons dribbling along the walls outside. The state funded this place, so even the litany-speakers in the waiting room sounded as if they had been filled with water. The facility's dolorous announcer didn't seem to mind.

"It can be genetic," the nun said.

The blood continued to gather.

"Where did you intern?" I asked. "Can I ask that?"

"Here at County," she said.

"Seminary?"

"Second year."

A crew raced by outdoors, canticles ringing sluggishly after. I could feel the doors to other confessionals sucking shut. They seemed the only things noiseless here, their basso pulses alternating like the padded valves in a sanctuary organ— a broken one, anyway.

She released my hand—the vial had taken its fill, so she snapped it into her console. Behind the screen, her device stuttered its ideas onto a readout. Since I didn't know how I'd earned my symptoms, I couldn't actually confess. The diagnostic machine sighed its irritation through decelerating fans, and its vents tsked themselves shut. I imagine that it didn't enjoy hunting for heresy. This box was called a confessional, after all—in an ideal world, triage would take care of itself.

"How long have you had the fever?" she asked.

"Since last night..." I struggled to remember, "... since the park. I must've slept in the park."

I watched headgear descend upon glinting wires—it swung suggestively before my neck. A tangle of sensor-pads followed.

"If you'll apply the pads," she said, swiveling on her stool, "we'll get started."

I had already picked the adhesive backs off of the first two. "What do you think it is—what's wrong with me?"

"I can't say," she said, flipping pages. "The reverend will have to analyze your Douay-enceph."

I could hear static fizzing as she powered up her monitor.

"The electrodes in the unit will deter any more hives," she offered.

Smearing the last pad across my left temple, I reached for the headgear. "What should I expect in here?"

Someone gargled a cry outside. I could feel the door-seal tightening.

"The unit will govern motor function," she said, wrapping her fingers around my wrist again. "The enceph needs to run you through a few simulations to see what might have caused your reaction—I'll monitor your levels out here."

I tried to get comfortable.

November 10, 6:47 PM—

Things were flapping in the dark. Someone had yanked the confessional's simulatory fingers from my head and neck—the stool lay on its side a few inches away. They had opened the door.

"He's got the same problem," Pitro said—I couldn't hear him very well over the screaming. Gwen clamped her hand over my mouth, and things quieted. The infinitesimal vacuoles creating space in my cells felt as if they had been inflated with steam. Even the smallest partitions of my awareness were sucking at each other—a great horde of gravity wells all competing to be the last.

"We'll have to get him to County," Gwen said, tracing a scalding finger across my forehead.

Pitro jammed a hypo into my neck. "We'll leave him in the park."

Gwen's blood began pooling upon my tongue. She didn't seem to have noticed—I suppose I'd been gnawing on her fingers.

"Will he remember?" she asked. My tongue swelled and choked away the last of my screams. She tucked her hand against her chest.

"Just enough," Pitro said. "We'll get him back—it's past time he joined us."

"To think," Gwen said, retreating into the dark, "his son."

"At least he survived."

November 10, 6:20 PM—

I held Gwen's hand fiercely—there was sap between her fingers, and I could feel it clinging to my foliated palms. She called for another sacrifice, and the men in the antler-headdresses clacked into action—they dragged another virgin onto the pyre. Women in toga-looking dress-things sang and wobbled. Someone shouted something unintelligible.

Gwen turned—though the confessional's simulator had smeared iridescent paint across her face and made of her hair an autumnal bouquet, she still resembled her regular, brunette self enough that I hadn't become totally disoriented. As ridiculous as it looked, I liked that she glowed.

"You order one," she said, tossing her head at the pyre.

I shook my head—I had antlers as well, only mine weren't attached to a hat, so I felt as if I might fall over.

"It's not real," Gwen said, smirking.

"Real enough."

She squirmed against me. "That's the point—you can't crack the Register without playing god."

I shook my head again. "Listen, I'm here about my father."

She studied me for a minute, suddenly demure.

"All right," she said, "there are parts that don't involve burning people."

I swallowed. With a nauseating whirl, the pyre disappeared, and the simulation digitized into a fallow field. The people sat in a circle around us now, keening and swaying—some were beating on drums. The simulation, I realized, had taken Gwen's divine clothing, and she laid now in the trough between two soil rigs. It had taken my leaves as well—though it had left the damned, unbalancing antlers. My skin began to itch, but I couldn't stop myself—it felt as if the simulator was making grabs at my brain. I settled into the furrow.

"Your father came to escape the Register as well," Gwen said.

"But he was clergy," I said, face buried in her neck.

"Who better, then?" she said. "He's a saint here."

The simulation knew its business well, but as I smeared the paints across Gwen's skin, I could feel the moonlight burning my shoulders. Something was wrong. The Register was clear:

sex carried biohazards. The simulation, it seemed, was full of allergenic sin. Never mind the dirt and the people and the acidic moonlight, I needed a mandate for this, and in most codices, that meant marriage.

I didn't even know Gwen.

She gestured, but I didn't need instruction—Register or not, I at least knew how sex was supposed to work.

As I found my way, she curled her legs around my hips with what sounded like a very real exhalation—I remembered the murmurs babbling through the hallway.

My joints felt as if they'd grown tired of holding things together. I screamed, shuddering into a convulsion.

But it doesn't count, I reasoned, the lines of various codices scrolling behind my eyes. It isn't real.

November 10, 6:00 PM—

I examined the address and double-checked my screen—the numbers matched, so I tucked the int-card inside my father's journal. The card's silicon edges winked as the journal closed over them—the screen powered down immediately after, taking the shine of the semi-gilded pages with it.

A plain-faced brunette answered my knock. Smiling, she tucked a ribbon of errant hair behind her ear. I noticed that she had strange, circular scars on her temples. It looked as if she'd irritated her skin with acid.

"Hello," she said, folding her arms.

I tucked the journal into my pocket. "Hey. I'm looking for the Stigmatics."

An older, elbow-patched man joined her in the doorway. Though he wore his hair as long as she did, he didn't seem to care that it had escaped the backs of his ears. His scars looked considerably older.

"I'm sorry," he said, frowning, "who are you?"

I glanced at them alternately. "Look, I just...my father mentioned Stigmatics in his journal, and I hoped I could ask—"

"Your father?" he said, shouldering past the brunette.

I wished I could talk to her instead. "Yeah, he was a reverend-doctor at County, but he died before—"

Elbow-patches lifted a hand, so I shut up. He studied me for a minute and then waved me in.

"You'll find your answers in the box," he said, smiling now. "You should see how it works—your father helped us build it."

I stepped inside, swallowing, and managed a weak smile at the brunette. She returned it shyly.

"I'm Gwen," she said.

Elbow-patches gestured us brusquely onward. "I'm Pitro."

I moved as directed. "You knew my father?"

Pitro grunted. "We all did, Mark—some, like Gwen here, only know him second-hand."

"How do you know me?"

Pitro marched us down a domino-tiled hallway. It looked to me like these Stigmatics, whoever they were, trafficked in confessionals—they lined the corridor evenly, dark, burnished, and crawling with iconography.

Pitro stopped before one and picked open an interface panel —the bas-relief cherub that had concealed it left only his stumpy legs to the task as Pitro punched commands into its grid. I could hear some faint, rising murmur around me, so I glanced at the other confessionals, but they looked inactive. I assumed someone had come by and played with all of their cherubs as well.

"In you go, son," Pitro said, gesturing to one of the now-open doors. Gwen ducked wordlessly into the other side, so I shrugged out of my jacket and stepped in.

"Put the pads behind your ears and on your temples," Pitro said, busy with the grid again. "I'll assume you can figure out the headgear for yourself."

I inspected the equipment—it dangled from monofilaments near the screen dividing the confessional. The leather padding on the small stool had chapped beneath too many visitors—its spongy flesh now showed through the gaps. The confessional looked like any other I'd seen. I was glad Gwen—and not some irritated facility cleric—was occupying the other side.

I could hear her powering up a monitor.

"Look," I said, "My father—"

"Your father tried it too," Pitro said.

The door closed, and the air tightened as a quiet seal inflated along the jamb.

With a sigh, I took hold of the pads.

November 7, 12:00 AM—

I shook the rat from the trap. Mom's humane neurophagic euthanizers hadn't been working. Steel and springs, I realized with a grimace, still did.

I shuffled backwards across the joists, palms slipping on the old house's vacuum bladders—at least the insulation worked. There just wasn't any way to keep the rain out with these wooden shingles—relics that they were.

After I deposited the newest corpse into the pile by the stairs, I went for the last trap—I'd tucked it under Mom's curio, where she kept the data-cards and textbooks and inoculation-shunts that County had delivered from Dad's office. I'd looked through them once or twice, hoping to find Dad in his old tools.

The curio-trap had yet to seduce a rat, so I wiggled out from behind it. When my hand brushed something slick between the cabinet's broken-toed feet, I thought maybe I'd forgotten one of the euthanizers. I recoiled, slamming my fist against the damned cabinet. The last thing I wanted was to lose feeling in my fingers for the evening.

There was no euthanizer—it was a book, so I extracted it, cursing, and scooted across the insulation. Moonlight was falling through the attic's vent in crawling globules.

The title page claimed the book had been my Dad's journal. Stunned, I read the first un-smeared page I could find, which was the last—I guess it had been upside down on the floor.

> . . . *The dinner party will be with a pair of my old fraternity brothers, the journal read,—some of those odd fellows from Cognition. I've filled their strange request for the sake of past rites. County will deliver the de-commissioned confessionals to their estate in a few days.*

I turned the page:

> *I'll bring my Registers—their request. I hope this debate*
> *will be as lively as the old synth-and-scotch days—now*
> *that they're calling themselves Stigmatics, I can only*
> *imagine it will be. This "temptation" of theirs: I imagine it*
> *will be anything but.*

Lying on my back, wet and moon-splotched, I fished my card out of back pocket. My heart raced as I jabbed commands into its grid. It had to find something.
What had tempted him?

Sweet Water

$\mathcal{S}$WEET WATER FOUND IT, BUT THAT'S NOT HOW WE remember things.

We remember it the way you're supposed to. The tradition of men in the wilderness, finding themselves in Great Things. Joseph Smith and the Golden Plates, Buddha and the Banyan Tree. The burning bush. A man named Christophorus. Because, of course, finding is simply seeing things correctly.

What makes a Great Find, though, is confusion. Great Men don't find anything when they know exactly what's going on. I was confused. Sweet Water wasn't. Which was why we rarely let her decide anything.

I was a better choice.

It was in a woodland. Which made sense. We spent a lot of time hiding in woodlands then. Sometimes, they were aspens, with their jack-of-the-wood eyes, their black eyes, staring, staring. Or graying spruce. The sweating mimosa. Cyprus. Sycamore. Pine. Joshua trees and persimmon orchards. We knew ourselves by the trees around us, a different people every time. Trees became monuments, druidic things without explanations. They had only functions.

We did better there than we had on the grasslands, or in the breadbasket, or up the mountainsides. We moved and moved, a different species of tree per year, zodiacally. You can measure fortune by trees when you can't risk the open stars.

Sweet Water found it in a coastal woodland. And we were post oaks, and sawtooth elms, and magnolia trees. We'd been safe here throughout the fall. There were other groups around, not far, but by this point we were mostly done with trading murders—our old diplomacy, sacrifices that kept everyone feeling strong. The idea being we could kill everyone if we wanted to.

She found the salt spring in a depression, where Great Things usually are: belowground. In the underworld. The trees ringed the spring's ferrous-soiled lip, a gap of twenty yards between them and the waters. They would not go down the slope. Where the waterline rose and fell (down now), the soil looked volcanic—sharp and ashen and thick with the grays and whites of alkali mud.

The water was red, scabbed along the shore, where it tongued the bad soil. The water was dried on its own surface, because what choice had it but to lap at what was there?

A pond named Tantalus.

Sweet Water was standing in it, the bunched ropes of her hair like serpents down her back. The soft hair on her thighs fanned on the surface of the water, reddened.

Of course, this is why I had wandered. I was looking for Sweet Water, not paradise. The truth of the whole thing is that I was never looking for anything else.

She looked like someone else standing there. The water had dyed her skin and her hair. She'd bathed, and it left her rouged. She looked candied, with the spring's salt glaze along the gaunt lines of her shoulders and upon her narrow fingertips, hanging.

I screed into the depression, could smell the burn on the air. It was hot here.

She was a blood-dried effigy, a daughter of the red mother liquor. I didn't know such names—what you called brinewater after its salt precipitated. But eventually, there were enough of us. Someone knew, so we knew. Someone knew something about everything.

I couldn't know then that she was play-acting the future. Looking bloody like that.

The hair beneath her belly winked with salt, in oxidized curls. A sculpture's hair. We no longer had a life for plucking and trimming, for taming a body's secrets.

And I didn't want them between us anyway.

"It's a brine spring, Salis," she said.

That wasn't my name. Not then.

"Can I come in?" I asked.

She turned her vinegar-fly gaze back onto the center of the spring.

"You don't have a choice," she said.

———

Father was salt. He was not gray salt or red salt. He had no saltpeter chunks, no natron skins. He was pure—the carefully gathered, the refined, the heights salt could achieve. Fleur de sel, white-on-white, flos salis.

But his eyes were as red as the brine beneath his heels. Everything he looked upon, including me, was red. He could see that everyone should be red. His children, born of Mother Liquor's water.

People should be red, or they aren't "people." Instead, they are the peat salts—the northern, the Celtic, the bay salts. Anything but pure. They were the Civil War ashes, cutting salt to stretch it further. Which was a crime in the Confederacy, not far from this woodland. Back then.

Even I knew what was to be done with criminals. What had always been done. Even so long ago, before Everything changed. Before it all Happened.

"Paradise," we remember Father saying, "begins with power."

He gleamed in the open sun. A great, living figurine, like those carved straight from the salt mountain, so long ago, by dirty Cardona workers. He was Lithuanian Roguszys—a spirit in a pickle jar. He was Saint-Guénolé, God's own eye, peering down on Le Bourg de Batz. Watching the salt marshes—their workers, the paludiers. They remembered still, in that land, the language of Vercingetorix. Even up to the First World War.

We had to realize that Father had always been all things to all people.

"Power," Father continued, "is the control of resources."

Father was *flos salis*, whom even Roman Cato had known. A resource, its acquisition, and its control. The holy trinity behind every war. He was even menstruation, our women *en salaison*—curing in salt. Fermenting, as they thought so long before Everything Happened.

That meant He was Sweet Water.

That meant He was me. In a salted state. "Salax," back when Pliny and Cato were still doing the thinking.

That is to say, in love.

"Resources begin, of course, with food, water, and shelter."

Of course.

"Shelter includes control not only of weather and predation, but of one's enemies as well."

I stood in Mother Liquor, becoming red—washing from the feet up. Like a disciple of Christ and what he did to people, who were the salt of the earth. Always washing feet.

"I will give you everything you need," He said.

I took Sweet Water's hand. The two of us in the same spring silt, now of the same red mud. A man and a woman made of earth, sharing a rib. As the red earth became flesh and Father exhaled His living breath.

Father who gave us everything we needed. Who gave us paradise.

Even if we forget that He had to build it first.

I knew Sweet Water before Everything Happened. I was confused even then. I borrowed great sums of money, student loans, to map, exactly, along which academic lines my confusion lay. I knew everything about it—I was an instructor of the misunderstood, and I worked middling jobs teaching this in beautiful, mind-altering ways. I published papers on the topic, and attended conferences, where we could all misunderstand each other together. Where we could be only discourse, which is far better than trying to mean discourse.

My boyhood came from manicured lawns, and Little League teams. Church membership and foreign exchange programs. I started out white, even if Father couldn't see that.

I worked by semester, working by credit cards, and loan payments, and buying nothing for my efforts. I had come from a modest suburb, and I had become confused. Because what they don't tell you is that such benefits can expire. I had done what I was supposed to, learned what I was supposed to, taught what I was supposed to. I was tolerance, and equality, and enriching the zeitgeist with a new cultural self, so we could correct the very language, the very thoughts, that produced selves who could not see the imbalances between different types of people.

And so. And carrying those suburbs, I looked fleur de sel. I looked flos salis. I didn't realize that it was part of the problem.

I had known Sweet Water before, and she had been the wrong color also. Had borrowed the same money and written the same papers and taught the same lessons to the same students. She had degreed her way to cultural enlightenment, too.

But Sweet Water was not confused. Sweet Water did not teach confusion. Sweet Water knew what flos salis really meant, and she didn't care about salary, or tenure, or temporary contracts. She was going to find the correct color, and learn to see it everywhere.

She was an expert.

Which is why we remember that I found the spring, and not Sweet Water. We make saints and martyrs of the innocent. It's better that way.

We had been together, on the campus, teaching our great tracts of nothing in different buildings, in different disciplines, even if we really were talking about the same things.

I knew her. We shared functions. Dinner parties. Intelligent discussions in coffee houses and at receptions where we pretended to listen to other people. We went to the same weddings, and the same hospitals, and the same personal tragedies. We visited the same coworkers' homes, who had given birth to the same children. All of them the wrong color, I would only, much later, realize.

When Everything Happened, I ran through the same crowds, past the same news-feeds. I ignored the same university-sent emergency-situation text messages that climbed into phone after phone, their digital fingers slipping into ours.

Everything will be okay, the little texts said, and it is good not to be alone.

I found her, and we ran together. I found her because I wanted to panic together. I wanted to continue seeing what made her trompe l'oeil.

She had eyes like green opals.
"Sweet Water," I said then.
She had eyes like a willow tree, and we hid there first.
"Follow me," she said.
And I will make you fishers of men.

God, of course, had something to say about Father. And Ruby passed it along.

Hark, the sound of holy voices,
Chanting at the crystal sea
'Alleluia, Alleluia,
Alleluia,' Lord, to Thee:
Multitude, which none can number,
Like the stars in glory stands,
Clothed in white apparel, holding
Palms of victory in their hands.

It was one of the few books we had. A Baptist Hymnal from 1885. From not so long after the Confederates and their salt crimes. Not so long after the need to distinguish between "Southern" and "Not" Baptists. They'd disagreed over what color people should be. Or they weren't people. Father had known this. I had known this.

Only people are allowed. This is crucial to building paradise. To finding it. You can't think of non-people as people. It complicates things.

We found the hymnal in a church, which had been sacked by a rival congregation, according to the graffiti on the walls. This was very common. The old book had approached us carefully, afraid when we called and whistled and settled on our haunches— our hands, like plates, extended. Our palms appropriately up.

Ruby skipped ahead. There were gaps in the old book.

They have come from tribulation,
And have washed their robes in blood,

This was what God had to say about Father, only He couldn't say it Himself. He couldn't say it through prophets or burning bushes, or political action committees. He'd said it through song, which is the greatest vetting. All of the Greatest Things have been remembered in song.

Hymns were choose-your-own divine adventure. A series of do-it-yourself beatitudes, with notes to play by number, that all the sons of man could pick up and sing, could remember, when the time was right. Like now. God, of course, having been divine enough to mean all things in everything He said. Even in everything we said. The devil was in the details, where it was best not to go.

It was difficult to tell what Ruby did and didn't believe. He was the hymnal's keeper, to be sure. I think that's what was most important. I didn't know if he Believed or not, but there were others of us, and they cared more that he said these things (someone had to), so he was ordained to the task by default—our bearded planchette, playing Ouija with his few, decrepit books. Aside from a Bible, I wasn't certain exactly which other books he had.

He spent most of his time with pieces of burnt timber, charcoaling things out of the books, their pale bellies exposed in love or submission. He corrected them. Working out just the right divine message for dirty people chasing food in the trees.

We were back in the camp, Sweet Water and I. Not everyone understood what Father had meant, by being in that spring.

"Everything begins with salt," Sweet Water told them. "We can cure food."

This was important. Winter was coming.

"We can make salves," I added.

A wind soughed through the camp, lifting our scraps of tarpaulin from their deadwood frames. Opening and closing the wedges of darkness, which were our doorways in. Normally, only we opened and closed them—they did not do this by themselves.

We were in a hollow beneath the trunks of our sassafras copse. It was a sinkhole, one of us knew, softened and grown over these many years past.

That should have been our first clue.

We listened as the leaves rattled. When we were sassafras, we knew to freeze when the leaves rattled. They made good cover for other things, approaching things on the noisy woodland floor. We stared animal-distances, into nothing-places, listening the way herds do. When the first of us ran, the rest of us would, too.

We could smell ourselves in the sinkhole, on the wind. Nothing smelled out of order.

Ruby thought for a minute, the ropes of his fingers working the spine on his hymnal. "Other people will want the salt."

That was the thing.

Missy scratched at her side. I thought of Sweet Water, where Father had implanted that first rib.

We called her Miss. She was the youngest of us. She sometimes sat with Ruby, pointing where and where things should be crossed out of the books, with the charcoal. She behaved like a Believer, but there were parts, there were songs, she didn't like. Ruby's books were afraid of her, and they trembled to keep from running away.

She and Sweet Water were the strongest of us. She and Sweet Water were not confused. They knew how to find things.

Miss had dirty eyes, and a dirty gaze, and she looked at everything. Always.

She had killed the most. But she still listened to me, like they all did. Since those early days, when that life had still offered the luxury of ideas. Like democracy. When I was voted into power because I was like each of them, without being anything particular myself.

"That's the point, Ruby," Sweet Water said.

"That's part of the point," I said.

Miss folded her narrow arms across her narrow chest. "We want them to want it."

Ruby's caterpillar brows inched together. "Why?"

"Power is the control of resources," I said.

Sweet Water and Miss smelled like sassafras, when they looked at me then.

There were already a few of us when we found Miss on a stretch of the old Interstate 20, in Mississippi. Which is how we named her.

Sweet Water and I were first, the two of us moving, moving. It didn't take long to realize there were things we couldn't do ourselves. Ruby had come next.

People still had guns then, though they were running out of ammunition. The idea had been to hoard it. To rise to power on bullets alone, but that hadn't worked. There had been too many people to shoot at. Too many shooting back. Bullets had picked up minds of their own, and they ran in lemming-herds any direction they could. You knew them by their gibbering, and they were difficult to understand, once they started their stampedes.

We still had gas then, though most vehicles were busted or burnt up. Pushed too hard, too long, by people who needed them to be more than machines. To get them away.

People had tried to hoard gas, too.

We had to stop because Miss had laid barbed wire across the highway. With the tires flayed, she killed the first of us by throwing a bottle of rags and gasoline through the back window. The person she hit did not have a name, we later taught ourselves.

We could have helped that person, but there was too much to risk. There was ourselves, who we couldn't let burn. If we had put her out, she wouldn't have burned.

Outside the van, when Miss tried to kill Ruby, he broke her nose against the asphalt. And her knives came spilling from her coat, and they were red. They blinked at us in that sunlight, squinting against our phosphene silhouettes where we were reflected on their surfaces. Clearly, Miss knew how to care for small things. For frightened things.

Those knives were just the color we were looking for. Red even then.

We talked to her while that other one burned.

———

Sweet Water and Miss left the camp. They came back, from that nearby town—what remained—with rakes and trowels, which were ready to do our work. Father's work.

The women said there weren't many people in the town, which was probably true. Those who could move on already had. Those who couldn't were simply branches on the forest floor. The bullets, in their great herds, had gone extinct, and enough of us had died that we didn't compete so much for what we needed.

We set the tools to work, scraping and raking—harvesting the salt from the spring. We gave the tools food and shelter in exchange for this work, but, of course, they weren't people. Soon, we wouldn't see them at all.

When we were Phoenicians, we figured this process out.

We left behind our precious coast, left behind its fish, like fish ourselves, testing our missing-link legs for the first time—going inland. Our city of Sfax was not so far from those reaching desert beds. From those sometimes-dry places and their great, salt plains.

But always we went back to the water, back to Sfax, dragging and gathering ourselves, just like the salt from its sands. And we waited again for fresh saltwater and the slow precipitation.

Others of us had waited before, in the same way around Lake Yuncheng, while others of us were still figuring out pyramids—even though we had, in those Egyptian sands, figured out how to drag and gather just the same. A world away, awakening to the same salt call. Listening to the same Salt Father, even if he carried other names then. Even if his name was wadi. Even though we called him Sebkha, and his breath of life, given in beds of golden dust, Natrun.

We learned to cut the mortal cord, then. To free our mummified rulers to eat in the afterlife. And we did this to the youngest of us. To the Living Image of Amun. To his dead throat with our holy knives. We learned to sleep in natron, to eat it, to become Salt Fathers ourselves, lying those seventy days in salt, our brains scooped away by priests' hooks. The best of us in tombs that had cost the lives of most of us.

We figured it out again, here, with our new tools. How to drag what we needed from the red water. We watched Mother Liquor, her floating algae scabs. We watched Her lap at Father's Salts while the magnolia winds blew.

Really, we didn't know what it was like for other people. We began running on principle, Sweet Water and I, because we had everything to get away from. We had the debts, and the all-but-aborted tenure tracks, and the meaningless bounce from thing to thing. Really, it had been a chance to get something going for once.

Mostly, people just went away. What we knew about the murders we heard from other people—those few we didn't flee from, simply because we didn't want to talk to them. Sweet Water and I were re-enacting faculty retreats and hiking trips. When we tried to pretend in groups that we could be something other than writers and researchers. Mostly, it worked.

Sweet Water and I were simply done with it all. As most others were. Really, I think that's what made Everything Happen. People just walked away. They stopped getting paid, and it didn't end with their jobs.

Bullet wranglers, and church-burners, and city-state builders were around, to be sure. But they had been around before. They just took up the new spaces left behind. It was hard in some places, like Mississippi, but where we were—that particular spot—had been hard before. We talked to Miss, convinced her to come along not because she could kill, but because she had the energy to. Which was hard to come by—for most people, those we saw, it was all they could do to read books on bean farming and generator repair. It was all others could do to repair dams and turn their homeowner's associations into something more serious.

There were other kinds of people. We were tree people, but there were mountain people, and lake people. There were highway people, who used roads like old rivers to open the veins of new business.

But most were gone, had run away, like Sweet Water and I.

There were no mutants. What gangs there were had existed before. I hadn't heard of any warlord kingmakers, or of any New Ethnic Empires. People killed each other, like we did, but, really, they'd done that before. Mostly, we stabbed on impulse when we surprised each other in the trees. Miss, I think, was never surprised, but it really didn't seem to matter if she killed a few people. We had rules, which I'd enacted, about killing others in our group. No one did that. We didn't have much need for other rules.

Really, we only started accepting others, Sweet Water and I, because we needed them. Not to bear arms in phalanx against other barbarians. Not to divide and conquer. We needed them because some things are difficult to do between only two people.

It was all right to be confused. I think it was the new spirit of the age. What the hell was the point? Where were we going? Sweet Water and Miss, they weren't confused, had never been, but that's because they were looking backward, at what came before. What they'd do with knowing it.

Sweet Water kept me from being alone. I didn't have loans anymore. I didn't worry about what it meant to come from where (from what). I didn't care anymore about balancing the representative discourse of the age. Because there was really only me. Sweet Water and everyone else being my own thoughts about them because, after all, you can't get someone in your brain. You can't know them. That was always something no one ever paid attention to, looking at me and having ideas about what it meant to be someone like me.

Sweet Water was the point. And that was nice, because she wasn't alone either.

But this isn't how we remember things.

Really, this isn't the way things were.

You have to remember, most of the others didn't come until later. Until after Father had built the paradise he promised. A modern-day Taghaza, a city built of salt, transplanted from the Western Sahara and straight into what remained, where we were, of the old U.S. Even Pliny had seen buildings made of salt in Old Egypt, and he and Father had talked often. It was not a new idea—building civilizations out of resources.

It wasn't long before Ruby decreed that we needed a Salt Chapel. We remembered that the miners, in Polish Wieliczka, had done so. Had carved one belowground. The underground omphalos, where faith and resources came together.

I didn't mind because, by this point, we'd expanded from simply caring for rakes and trowels. Now we had boilers and sifters, hammers and nails—tools upon tools for collecting Father's salt. And then there came the livestock, the needles, the beeswax and the lime. All the tools that wandered, apprehensively, back down our salt trails, back to the source. The first American roads were merely widened footpaths, traced from the routes animals wandered in their quests for salt. Before we paved them. So we could die more easily, at greater speeds, in traffic accidents. Of course, we had mirrors for looking backward. At what had come before. But they didn't help.

And we cared for all these wandering tools. Some of them got to be people, based on value. Ruby kept them busy. Kept them in place, so I didn't mind.

But some tools just aren't necessary for harvesting and trading salt. These we turned away, and they were becoming angry. Enemies. In India, before Gandhi had started his salt revolution, we'd solved this problem with a thorn hedge. A 2,500-mile customs line cultivated from prickly pear and acacia and bamboo. It kept smugglers out. We used one to keep away the not-people.

We weren't tree people anymore. We were salt people. We had tamed fires, like sheep, to heat the boiler-pans, and because we knew so many trees, knew them so well, we domesticated them, too. We told them "stay," and they did, while the fire took hold, shyly, and burned them to boil the salts from their brine.

———

Everything had been Happening for a while. Before.

Sweet Water had paid someone at her salon to put beeswax in her hair. They created false dreadlocks, which she bound in an oversized ponytail against the back of her head with a band of cloth—something stitched in Orissa. Fair trade. Organic hemp. Or something.

Like I said: for a while. Things didn't just Happen.

We had conversations like this:

"What do you think?"

One dread dangled free, by design, from the corner of her hairline onto her shoulder. It looked like a finger.

She looked upward, thinking, still chewing. Fork suspended. "Pre or post?"

I'd made lamb tips over couscous. "Whichever. Both."

Now she had an answer. Hid it behind her gaze, planting it on the plate. "Well, it resists a normative paradigm. Post doesn't mean anything. It all happened before."

Acid jazz tinned softly from the mp3 dock in my living room. Cars sounded like come-and-go rain as they whispered down my suburban block. My front door window was a mosaic of leaded glass, so the passing lights were just glowing shivs, trapezoids and other sharp things, in my six-by-ten feet entryway. My foyer.

We were both experts.

"In Sweden, girls used to make porridge," I said. "They'd salt it and go to sleep, thirsty. The men who brought them water, in their dreams, was whom they'd marry."

"Yes," she said.

"But it's too early. To talk about that."

See?

Primarily, the reason the spring was red was because of the brine shrimp. The springs in this area were high in concentrations of Dunaliella salina, pink micro-algae. It's high in beta-carotene, which protects the algae from the bright, white light. The shrimp eat the algae. This is why flamingos are pink—because they eat the shrimp, unless they were zoo-raised, and then they were fed canthaxanthin, which was a pigment used in illegal tanning pills. Farm-raised salmon were fed the same thing. To be sure they were the correct color.

But Mother Liquor was red, too, for different reasons. After Father precipitated himself from the brine, to take form and speak, the fluid wasn't brine any longer. Then it was Mother Liquor, and she was still red, her shrimp and algae long since leached of their colors by the acquiescent trees, who accepted the tamed fires, to boil the fluid out of the brine. To reduce it—Mother for Father.

For a while, we kept boiling Mother away. It wasn't until Ruby blessed the spring, and we sent the pick-axes and sluices and backpacks down underground, into the salt veins themselves. It wasn't until then that we had any eucharist.

We didn't know why Mother remained red. But it didn't matter.

Ruby led us in a hymn that day. An old one, which he'd reconstructed from the crippled hymnal's moldering pages. He'd had to wash many of the pages with quicklime to kill the book lice, so there weren't many charcoal-line-edits anymore. He'd reset the splintered hymns, in their correct forms, from memory. The little book was proud and clean, and it responded well to strangers now.

> *There is pow'r, pow'r, wonder working pow'r in the blood*
> *of the land*

I wasn't sure what he was leaving out. None of the others seemed to care. Sweet Water didn't care. Neither did Miss, or any of the trowels we'd promoted to people. Or the hammers-and-nails. Or the knives.

> *There is pow'r, pow'r,*
> *wonder working pow'r*
> *in the precious*
> *blood of the land*

Ruby came at us with a tarnished chalice. It sloshed, full of Mother. Father had been filtered slowly out, by hand, and placed back into the spring.

Ruby's cheeks were already red as he came over. To me first.

"This is the blood of the covenant."

The little, clean Bible looked pleased, flapping in the shade with the hymnal, and some of the newer books.

"Do this in remembrance of me."

It didn't take long to become the correct color, ingesting Mother like that. Like eating brine shrimp. More importantly, it didn't take long to cease being the wrong color, which was how we thought about it.

Sweet Water wasn't being idle, either.

With enough trowels, you can carve almost anything from salt. Quickly. Miss was good at finding dynamite. With Ruby's help, she recruited the nitrates and chlorides and acids. He sent his ever-growing flock of white-washed Bibles and hymnals and prayer books with her. And, escorted by the flashing herds of Miss's knives, the flock reconciled the differences between the chemicals. Convinced them to play along. To learn to love woodmeal.

With enough dynamite, you can carve almost anything even faster. The dynamites had no hope of becoming people. There was just no way, given their necessarily apocalyptic worldview. They were eschatological, whether they liked it or not, and once we sent them down, they weren't allowed to leave the mines. They had their children there, had chemical sex and shared meals in saltbox rooms they carved in their off time.

So, not only had we carved a chapel, we had baths, too. I found Sweet Water there most days, pickling in the hot waters. Preserving herself en salaison. Her red skin perpetually smooth. I wondered if Sweet Water, so long in salt water, would begin to reproduce. Parthenogenesis. Immaculate conception. It wasn't so long ago, on those ships overrun with rats and yersinia pestis, that we thought rats could reproduce without sex, simply by being in salt. Sweet Water was another vessel, too long at sea, too long in the salt. Likely to become more.

There had been moonlight on the lake that night, but not much else. We'd taken Sweet Water's vintage Yugo out. After watching an awful production of *Copenhagen* at the community theater. We supported such things, in the months between spring and fall semesters, by telling each other "For such a limited budget, it was an effective use of minimal light," and "The new director has potential." We'd finished half a terrible bottle of scuppernong wine, which we drank because Sweet Water had a sister in the Carolinas who sent it to her. We liked to support such awful things because we believed they had a place in an enlightened society. We believed they were a part of correcting normative discourse. Of deconstructing hegemony.

There wasn't anything on Sweet Water but moonlight either. Her clothes were in a pile next to mine on the shore.

Like I said, we were experts.

"Do you ever wonder about the point?" she asked.

"Of what?"

"Anything. Research. Articles. Conference papers. Cooking dinner."

It is difficult to converse while treading water.

"Sure. I guess."

"Sure."

She flashed her chest, not at me, but at the moonlight, backbending. "Some days it just feels like killing time."

We hadn't been at the university long, then.

"Are we wasting time now?"

"It's too early," she said, "to talk about that."

But her skin had all become one tone. There was no distinction anymore, except by touch, between lips, nipples, or elbows. If anything, it was too late. She'd never been confused about any of this. About articles, research, or the lowest APR between three cards.

The demand for salt had increased, and now, there was need for purity. For difficult salt. For a luxury that others didn't have, which meant it had to be purified.

We knew this necessitated fluids—either blood or beer—to clarify the salt. But we didn't have much beer. Miss was meeting with the Blood Father tomorrow, to negotiate. We would need a lot.

Livestock was for eating, not for purifying salt, after all.

There were sassafras leaves steeping in the bath around us. Sweet Water had eyes like blue-green algae, and I hid there now.

This was all okay.

The Blood Father had a daughter, who'd been Aztec. Vixtociatl, banished to the salt water by those who loved fresh water. Every year after that, one of the Blood Father's Aztecs stood in for Vix, who'd taught the people to harvest salt. The stand-in danced for ten days before they killed her.

So it was okay then, and it was okay now. We paid the Blood Father in salt, which seemed rather circular.

Ruby led a responsive reading that day, as the blood was escorted underground, to its new quarters. He'd patched the reading together and taught it to his others, who were no longer books or pages, but Rubys in their own rights:

By terrible things thou wilt answer us in righteousness.
Which stilleth the tumult of the peoples.
Thou visitest the earth and saltest it.

The salt we produced, in the end, was pure. We named it *flos salis*, and we traded it to our non-red allies, like the blue men fishing silver from the mountains. They were strange. They worshipped the silver, ate it, even, and it turned them blue.

Ruby used the chapel to inter the leaders of our enemies in the walls. He mummified them with dirty salt, and sealed them, semi-transparently, into their vaults with buckets of rendered fat and gypsum. We looked after the conquered belowground. In the mine. They became blood.

What was odd, though, was that these leaders looked just like people, after they'd been interred.

Once, we had traded the salt to the Hanseatic League, to the Genoans, and Venetians.

After that mob of unbelievers assassinated Joseph Smith, Brigham Young led the Mormons to the Great Salt Lake. They became the salt of the earth.

This was all okay.

I hadn't seen Father in such a long time. But I saw Mother every day. We called her Sweet Water, for we took pains to remove Father. To precipitate the union.

Because I'd been elected back then, when we had time for luxuries like democracy, I am remembered for this. I am remembered for the inalienable rights we manifested for all people. For our democratic nation. Our people and religion. I am remembered for Miss's gentle hand, tending her flocks, for Ruby's painstaking transcriptions. Saving herds and herds of Holy Writ, one re-created line at a time. I am remembered as the one who spoke to Father.

We purify more salt now than anyone, and sometimes we get together in one another's homes to tell jokes. To play games, and to sleep in the soft, suburban shells of our homes. Once per week, we put on our finest clothes and gather to hear what Ruby has to say.

Every night, before bed, Sweet Water puts lotion on her hands. She applies balm to her lips, and she reads for a few minutes, no matter how tired she is. Some nights, we sleep without touching, and the pecan trees make noise like come-and-go rain, when the wind blows.

Syntagm

E ARE FIFTEEN WHEN WE CREATE OUR FIRST LANGUAGE. It is a cipher, a tongue we make by altering our first language, which we did not create. Old words, new meanings. Things that appeal to adolescent poets, adolescent boys—long-haired flannel kids in corners who take more meaning from things like song lyrics than they should. Than is fair to the songs. Anthems and punctuations for the roil of being. Young.

In our first language, things come to mean otherwise. When we say Are you guys ready?, which means, primarily, ". . . to do something," we are saying, now, (especially now) We are all for one, which is a thing long-haired adolescents among the post oaks and greenbrier in the undeveloped acreage against Veterans' Park, twenty feet above the creek bottom, fists and rope-swings, around illicit sleepover campfires, and the rites of our first secret society, and over film canisters of pilfered loose-leaf tobacco curling smoke in pilfered fathers' pipes, and thoughts like small secrets of the girls we don't speak to, say to each other. It is a thing we say to each other. We create our first language from our first language, altering it into something that appeals to us. And now we mean "Are you guys ready?"

This is how we parse our thoughts. On things like how right the Romantics were, how right the landscapes and energies and expressions of self in creek beds, geodes, and mountainsides. Like what it is to be landscapes ourselves, which is a better thing to be than adolescents in used cars, west of Dallas, in a place without project housing, bars, or even public transportation. Like how much sense this (or that) song makes. Like how things are going to go down.

We are fifteen when we create this first language, which we call "No"—the collision of our names, the letters we share. We are cheating, of course, using a word from our first language to name our first language. This is important. It is important to us that our first language means something to someone beyond us. Even though we will not share it, are forbidden to share it, with anyone else. N and O are the only letters to appear in each of our names, but only in the ones we create. Danno's name is really Daniel, and it would share an E with Owen. Thompson is my last name, the one we use—Alan, which is my first name, would share an A with Daniel. No is what we want, because it is the real name of all things we have to say.

We say other things as well: Later, which is now. I know, which is My honor, my life. We mean things adolescently, which is the greatest way to mean them. The potential way to mean them.

She is part one of three: Love, Honor, and Truth—the three things we mean most, in that perfect order. We will only mean this now while she is only potential. When she becomes real, for each of us, all three things become just that one.

But not now. Or rather, only now, if one translates in reverse.

All of this is important, of course. For we create a second language. We are men then, and nothing means anything.

"We need a word for this," I say.

"Something that won't change—" Owen says "—doesn't mean change."

Danno doesn't like this cigarette business. The tobacco pipes at least come from our books: elf-land wizards, and poets strolling moors, and soldiers carrying swords, which is a fight we like. A fight we would have a chance in, when intelligence (and not simply bullets) has something to do with it. We tell ourselves. This is what we think. Pipe smoking is people thinking.

Still, Danno buys cigarettes for me and Owen because his father is in the same group as the man who owns the gas station and convenience store near the park. A Mythopoetic Men's Movement group. On occasion, Danno and his father and the man from the convenience store gather with other men, other sons, to channel themselves through ritual drumming. Through "talking drums," or sound boxes they make in their garages with wood glue and jig saws. They plumb archetypes by sharing classical mythology, and they read poetry by people like Robert Bly. They know about things like role stress, which Danno and his father have both encountered, individually, in therapy. I won't know what they are talking about until graduate school.

Once a month, my father and I go on Boy Scout campouts, which isn't the same thing.

This convenience store man sells cigarettes to Danno, but not to us. He is like that. Danno is like that.

We are in a copse of honey locust trees, back behind Danno's housing development, in undeveloped acreage, which we call home. It hasn't been developed because it is private property, and not for sale. We are trespassing.

Danno thinks of one of these trees, the crook-backed one, as a totem—a self he can control, a stronger self. One immune and apart from all of this. It is the oldest tree in the copse, the one that had taken lightning to half its limbs. We all call it Danno.

Danno leans.

"We'll call this 'now.'"

Which, of course, in reverse, means later.

And this is what he means. Now. Now means then. Nothing happened to us today. School is over for the week. We will be playing *Dungeons & Dragons* and going for hamburgers and drinking soda all night. But that hasn't happened yet. There weren't any fights today. There isn't any homework. We haven't talked to any of our girls. The ones, specifically, among all of them whom we can't talk to. Like I said: Love, Honor, and Truth. There are rules to this, and it is easier to follow them than to risk fucking things up.

Owen is doing just fine. Danno can't know what this means now, but he will know it later.

Which is exactly the point. We will always need now to mean exactly this. Later, now will mean so much more, once we know what a terrible thing it will be to capture this moment—what terrible meanings will happen to it because we are isolating it from all other moments. Making it vulnerable to all the meanings that will happen to it as all the first-language nows keep meaning (are forced to mean) now.

We do this to ourselves.

———

They were in Phoenix, which is where their father lived. Visiting.

"I was with him," Danno's sister said, tiny through my phone.

"What?" I asked.

"On the couch, watching T.V.," she said.

By themselves. Danno's father wasn't even in the room with them, because it was late. Which defeated the purpose.

"What?"

My wife walked into the dining room, where I was sit-standing. Walking and not. I thought of Danno's old house, so close to home. The sun room was nothing but windows, and that's where the talking drums and the sound boxes were kept, alongside fossil souvenirs from Galveston Bay. Hiking sticks, and the converted aquariums where the ball pythons lived.

"What?" she asked.

"So I called the ambulance right away," Danno's sister said.

"Wait."

I wondered if there were a sun room in this new house. This Phoenix house. Danno's father and step-mother had moved there while Danno and I shared a duplex, in college. Home no longer existed for him, in either language.

"Okay," I said, "what? I mean, which side?"

"The left," she said. "It's too soon."

"What caused it?"

"A blood clot in his leg, through a tiny hole in his heart."

Primarily, stroke means movement. Energy put (somehow) to use. Danno leaned, having taken his brain's electro-chemical lightning to half his limbs. He had grown this clot in the meat of his thigh, with each Friday-night hamburger—later, with each Wednesday night beer. He had nested it and warmed it and taught it the sound of his voice, while we walked and hiked and learned to sail. He had given himself to it in the stress of his first marriage, in the anti-depressants and internet dating services that followed. Danno was a clot of blood, and he had helped my wife and I pack up our everythings and move them nineteen hours away, when we took new jobs, one year ago.

"Is he?"

She was crying now. "They're concerned because it happened where the personality is."

"What. Can I talk to him?"

There were rules to this, a rite—a recreation of older times, preserving community knowledge, asking questions with idiotic answers, unnecessary answers. The questions were the point. Where? Which room? Phone number? Getting the story straight to tell it twenty times, getting closer with each phone call to making this normal.

There had to be a reason why I didn't ask these things.

"No."

I hadn't spoken to Owen since my wedding. We made a point of texting each other our new numbers each time we moved, so we wouldn't have to.

It is important, at this point, that we believe in God. Because, later, in college, we won't. For precisely this reason, because I am soon to disbelieve, it is very important that I make Danno and Owen believe.

Our ideas have to be realizations—they can't be self-generated. They have to come from divine order—a greater sense of how things should be. We learned Transcendentalism in our sophomore lit classes, and it is right. There is a here that we are missing, but so much less than everyone else. We find it in our favorite songs and at home and around the gaming table. There is no point in talking to our girls if they don't get this. This was why, of course, we don't talk to them.

This is as close as Danno gets to believing, so I convinced him to follow me to church. His father doesn't mind, though he disbelieves. Owen goes because he does everything I tell him to. I've been taught nothing but panic for my friends' immortal souls.

Our Sunday School class is specifically for high school boys. We learn, from our teacher who has done mission work in five countries, that women are not supposed to teach religion. She tells us that the Bible tells us so. This is chivalric, and we are fucked here by Honor and Truth.

I look at Danno, and he writes I know on his notepad.

Perhaps this is the beginning. We each write a poem about this, and they each appear in our school's literary magazine. We are on staff this semester. Two of our three girls are also.

Owen's is not.

By the time we reach our third year of college, we will have had the conversation that God is, in fact, the universe. That suns and orbiting planets and plasmoid dark matter are god's atomic structure. Perhaps, then, we are simply clots of tissue in God's great thigh. We know, after all, that we are cast in his image, that he gave himself to us.

We are getting somewhere, on our way to appropriate late-twenty-something ideas about faith and being nothing. We are becoming energy put to good use. Strokes, ourselves.

We will discuss God's great thigh while we smoke pot in our living room, which will be done up with fishing nets, dress forms, fencing foils, and the other emblems that we feel identify us as un-serious romantic individuals. By this point, Danno will have taught me how to play the sound box.

Eventually, she becomes real. We begin to talk. Owen and I each learn that it had all, really, always been about sex. Danno isn't dating anyone.

My parents are out of town this weekend, so after we swim, after we are in those next-step swim suits, we get ready for this. For the first time. She and I, finally. Before my phone rings.

"There's no one here with him," her mother says. Owen's girlfriend's mother.

"What?" I say.

"I think—he's panicking."

This is not about Owen's mortal soul.

"Wait."

"Could you come over here?" she asks.

"Have they been fighting?"

"Yes—not really. Owen chased him around the driveway. The police would rather not arrest him."

"What?" my girlfriend asks. She is ready, too.

He is a friend from junior high school. High school, too, but not as much. This has been coming on the side—a thing born of long afternoons while Owen was working with us. On the literary magazine. His girlfriend was left without options.

"Owen ran into the street," her mother says, "but the cars wouldn't hit him. They just swerved, or stopped."

Luckily, Owen has been coming with us to church, because I told him to. For this reason, the staff at the Thousand Oaks center are willing to admit him after hours. Because it is a religiously funded institution. I wait with Danno and Owen's mother in the waiting room while they process Owen in another room. I fall asleep in an arm chair, still in my swim suit.

We gave him a machete, that Christmas, because it was the closest thing to a sword we could find. We found a store in the mall that engraved it with "My honor, my life" in a font called "German Gothic."

He is not allowed to keep this.

"When can you talk to him?" my wife asked.

It was two days before his sister thought to call me again. There had to have been a reason why I didn't ask for the number the first time.

"I don't know."

"Do you need to go there?"

We couldn't afford a plane ticket to Phoenix. One month later, we would be back in Dallas, to participate in two weddings— friends from graduate school. This is what we did now: attend weddings.

After her, Owen impregnated a different girl. He married her. While Danno and I were in college, Owen moved to Texarkana to manage a seafood restaurant.

"I can see him in Dallas."

This is what was happening now. This is what we didn't realize.

"Do you know that he's been going to church," I said.

"What?"

"Because this girl, she goes."
"Wait. Maybe he's alone."
Alone didn't mean anything.
We had ceased to believe in college.
"The only thing worse would be if he had died."
"I know," she said.
"That's not what I'm talking about."

Danno leans. The stream below it is two inches closer per year, as the tree bows under its dead weight, aging. We have each carved a sigil of a bird into the collapsing bark. Our seals, with which we sign our letters and make things official.

"You know they'll make fun of us," he says.

One of these birds is not real.

"Whatever," Owen says. "they won't know."

I am supposed to be the smart one. "Of course. But secretly—I mean, come on—do you think they'd rather have poets and D&D geeks, or office monkeys with tie-jobs?"

We are talking about her, and we plan to meet all three of her at once—a convergence of two groups. We are only half-kidding when we talk about how crazy it would be if they simply came hiking down the creek bed, with rules of their own.

The plan is universal. We'll be neighbors, after college—or as close as will be manageable.

Danno shoves Owen as he launches from the creek-shore, fists rope-swing tight. "Yours is going to be the ugly one!"

"He wants to talk to you," Danno's sister said.

"Can he?"

"He wants to."

The name of his hospital is Thunderbird, in Phoenix. I was warned that this was most important to him. For now, this was his everything.

I heard him grunting on the other end of the line.

"Hey, asshole," I said. I was the one who could make him laugh.
He made a sound like a bird calling. A thunderbird.
"What?"
My wife's hand was soft against the back of my neck.
He choked. Made the sound again.
We are men, when we create our second language. I cannot transcribe it, via three-letter alphabetic keypads, into a text-message for Owen. There is a sound, from our past, that makes sense of this. We made the sound once, fifteen years earlier, calling to each other in code, through the trees. I will text it from our past selves to our present selves tonight. Starting with Owen. Because it will be easier.

I am not sure we are finished. Danno and I. When I hang up the phone. So I call out, just in case. One bird to another. SONARing space-time with sounds that don't exist.

Storm Chasing

$\mathscr{S}$TORMS SEND YOU THINGS. IT STARTS WITH RAIN, WITH WIND and green clouds. Sometimes hail, a tornado. Uprooted photinias and mangled street signs. The severed limbs of white elms and black oaks. A father. A son. Anything, really.

We lived in North Texas, near Dallas, where the metroplex gassed its own thermals and heat waves up, into the cold air, making storms of its own, even if we couldn't see them. You live in places like this because you want those storms. You want what they can bring.

I learned to keep still on our front porch, whenever I could dodge my mother's orders to descend into the basement, into the damp dark, under the old mattress that roofed my storm fort, my safe place where they could find me if things began to fall apart. I learned whenever I could stay out of sight long enough to get outside, where the storm sirens Dopplered across rooftops and soccer fields. When I could find my father, we kept still. He would lean against the pillars on the porch, the clouds from his pipe moving sideways, in two directions at once—just like the rain. Our dog sat at his feet, being very still.

I would stand there, too, listening, smelling, being still. Learning what it was men do in storms.

"Come in," my mother would say. "Come away from the storm."

But the storms would be inside, too. Small ones—the size of my basketball. They made puddles and small fires and slicks of ice where they went, and I chased them down into my fort.

The little storms' stains remained for years in the carpet. Like cat piss or soda. My father would shampoo them with a rented machine from the grocery store, but they always came back. Even after I left.

At eighteen, I started moving. First, out west. To go to school. West Texas is a world unto itself, a different land and language, a different faith than what grows in North Texas. The land and the air are both red with the dirt. The red earth that, not so long before, became done with all things. Became unhappy with the Great Depression and its farmers. Became unhappy with being earth and became, instead, the breath of madness. Bankruptcy. The earth became a storm, and the people called it a black blizzard.

My father had lived in this country. When he was a boy, his father worked for oil. But I did not go for my father or grand-father. I did not go to inherit the red of the earth, which, it seemed, was what men did. I followed a girl, and storms began searching for me.

When the first dust storm came, I learned from the television what to do. Stuff damp towels into the window frames, along the doorjambs. Stay indoors. Watch the earth gather in drifts, like dark snow, against retaining walls and upon sidewalks. Skip class and think about that smell, that cold chalk smell, which is the earth coming through the towels anyway and rising through your nose. God breathed life into the first man made of the red earth. Out west, it worked the other way around.

The earth came upon the city—a sunset, from the wrong direction, and it was strong enough to strip the paint from your car.

I couldn't go outside, to keep the tradition. To watch the storm—to at least see it coming, so I squinted into the peephole in my apartment's door and tried to remember the smell of tobacco.

I followed a girl.

"I've decided I want to buy cigarettes," I told her.

"What? Get away from the door."

"Cigarettes." I had smoked them as a teenager. I had smoked them in secret, on the private, wooded property abutting the municipal park. My friends and I stole them from our fathers, and we smoked them in circles. The way you do. Because we could never keep pipes burning.

But she didn't like them, so I stopped.

A dust storm makes your eyes water, even inside. Even hers, then.

"Are cigarettes more important than me?" she asked.

I didn't have a dog, either.

"Well, are they?" I asked.

This is what happens.

—⁓—

"It isn't easy," my mother told me.

I was the last to move out, and I am the only son. It was four and a half hours from my apartment out west back to my parents' home in the north.

Once, we painted door jambs with lamb's blood to protect our children. Today, it's easier to move them out of town.

"Things have been hard," she told me. My parents helped me move out west with two trucks, so they drove home in them both. A driver per truck. Nothing but cell phones between them.

"He had trouble with the lanes," she said, "on the way back. He was watching dust devils." He slowed down, creating distance between the trucks, so she couldn't see him. So he wouldn't look weak.

When he was a boy, out west, he and my uncle would play in dust devils. Jump inside and wake up ten minutes later, bruised and dirty between soil rigs.

But not anymore. She was worried.

—⁓—

We talked on the phone, still. He was working a lot, ingesting each small task like antibiotics. Straight into his bloodstream, where the stress could do things like change the fluid pressure in his arteries.

"I'll have results next week," he said. "Mom and I are hoping it's enough."

When I was a boy, he and I took small things apart. Crystal radios and remote control cars and model rockets. Particularly when it was raining. Things would fall with the rain, and the honey locust trees leaned in all directions with the wind. On the weekends, during Boy Scout campouts, he taught me to recognize trees. To name them.

"Right," I said. "Keep me posted."

"I envy you, son."

West Texas gets better storms than North.

I didn't stay in the west. Things fall apart in all places the same way. In the west, back north. Anywhere. There is not so much of anything that the wind cannot take it apart.

I didn't stay in the west, and neither did she. We were both going back. We had a bad habit of following each other.

A snow storm is the type people like best. With enough snow, all things cease. Schools, work, traffic laws. People are free to do what they like in the name of bad road conditions. And in the white, even loud things are made quiet. Every footstep has a point, because you want to hear it crunch.

Before we left, an ice storm fell upon the town and slicked the roads. It caused an unlikely traffic accident—cars propellering around each other to hit only mine. Within forty-five minutes, the sun had sublimated all of the ice away. The story became implausible. Insurance agents, and angry fathers, and eye witnesses called. I was too young for this, so I ingested each small thing. I tucked them away in the dark warm of my blood stream, where they could do things I wouldn't feel until later, as an older man, when I would need angioplasties and prostate exams to detect them.

But my insurance was stronger, with better lawyers. I had it because my father had served in the military. It was a benefit he earned for me.

My mother began storm chasing. She was trying to help. It takes a generation to learn these things, and she was in a hurry.

She acquired a faster truck, self-help books, and software that could index symptoms. She learned from other chasers what to watch for, what a downdraft meant when looking for storm sign. Storms develop patterns when something is wrong. Like people.

After I came back, she told me these things. I held her hand—all things from my mother—and I listened to her helplessness.

There wasn't much left. She showed him videos—what she'd learned during her chases. It was common for storm chasers to set their chase videos to a sound track and to edit them in ways that built suspense. She showed him the data, from the computer, what she'd indexed.

He agreed—something was wrong. Even he didn't know.

"That's when he started seeing them at home," she said.

"What?" I said.

"In the hallway. At night. The smallest storms, spinning and raining—the size of the dog. I found him once chasing one in the closet. Just sitting there, by himself."

He was creating distances like wormholes, from compacted spaces. He was looking for places to chase his own storms in secret. A highway to slow down upon, to create space, complete with dust devils.

But despite all of this, I was happy to be back. At night, in my new apartment, I listened to the wind and hoped every night to hear sirens.

———

There were quiet years. I knew we watched the same news casts. The same prime-time interruptions, with radar imaging. Super-Doppler and 4-D. We saw the same county maps in the same upper left corners of our screens, and we wondered, together, which counties were ours.

We watched the same tickers at the bottoms of our screens, waiting out the alphabet to see if our county was the center of the storm. If we were included in the tornado warning, in the severe thunderstorm warning, in the flash floods and the hail storms and the dangerous winds. We waited for these storms to bring us all things.

During the quiet years, he would call in secret. He had a new cell phone by this point, and my mother was no longer chasing.

He would call because it was something we could have—between only us. He would call with crystal radios and remote control cars and afternoons with model rockets in his voice. He would call to speak only in merit badges, and canoeing tests, and learning to build fires with only one match. He would call to remember now.

He had given up something. The dust devils along that west Texas highway. The landslides from the Northwest, which were foreign to us, but they were a part of his job: traveling to do business in strange places. He had given up monsoons on other continents, earthquakes, and leaving voice mails for himself about weather patterns.

I had not inherited the red earth in my lungs from living out west. I was a storm, bringing the past with the rain. But a father cannot be his own son. In the end, someone is either sacrificed or murdered, depending on who survives. The Bible tells us so.

I was in graduate school by this point. I was nights at the bar and too many books and not yet married. I didn't need to ingest anything. There were no pressure systems building polyps in my colon. There was no zoster rising through the water table of my soft flesh. There was nothing about me that could be called a storm.

Eventually, you become all storms. I arrived for my wife, having been nothing but wind for seven years, ever since that afternoon I followed my father home from the west. He had driven the moving truck full of many things—things he had bought so I would have possessions: a bed, a couch, a Zippo lighter. I had driven the car he had bought for me, away from the college he'd paid for me to attend, and I became nothing but directed movement as I watched tumbleweeds catch themselves in the cotton.

My wife had not chased anything. Had waited in place for the right time. Had not followed the wrong people to the wrong places. Which causes the storms to come after you, which means those you left behind must run after them. To receive all things from the wind.

I married her. There was nothing coincidental about any of this. But I had not finished with being westerly, and we moved together, even further east, to the Carolinas. As far as we could go before there was no reason to be wind anymore.

"Things aren't good," my mother told me again.

Even the earth in one's lungs can be moved by the wind. It takes a long time, but it happens.

———

He began to find storms everywhere. Not only alone, in the closet, but at work. At church. He found them during afternoon trips to the car wash. My mother would tell me when she found rain puddles on the carpet or hailstones in the cereal box. She would collect the mail. Letters from the snow and the wind. From the black blizzards. She would open them to discover nothing but dark sand.

When I was a boy, my father and I went on our first campout with the boy scouts. It stormed all weekend, so we sat in the tent and made pancakes over a one-burner camp-stove. Once, we camped in a snowstorm, and my fingers became so weak, I had to ask my father to help me undo the buttons on my jeans.

He had taught me what it is men do during storms. But now I didn't know how to tell him.

How Nothing Happens

IT'S STRANGE TO LISTEN IN, KNOWING AT ONCE NOTHING AND everything about the discussion.

"Have you been having trouble?" she says. The only woman. She wears a pant suit and lacks a face. She has a face, but it remakes itself instant-by-instant. Or my recollection of it fails at that speed.

There are three others in the room, beside me, but I'm not sure yet who's projecting whom here. So either they count or I do. But not both. Some of us are selves as ignorance, somehow making this up, systemically—it fits on its own, but it's like watching a television show with the wrong audio track. At least it might be. It's what happens when you have too many people making what's real. *Networking*, they call it.

We'll call one of the others here Rashail, for I can now recognize his dark complexion. That name is appropriately complected, and since I don't know—or haven't realized, or haven't created—the lines of his heritage, he has none. A name will work well enough.

"I've been having trouble," he says, with more face than she. He's a little more connected to this room, this moment, than she seems to be.

"Me too." We don't care about « this one. His voice will suffice. Maybe he's just calling in.

"I haven't been able to get in since this weekend," the third one says—a blond, typically attired, 1980s office-worker. The problem they're all discussing here has to do with keeping buildings operating. Also signs, telephone poles, mailboxes. The things we use. Their job is to keep all these things happening. Sometimes things go wrong, inside them.

I'm taking notes for the meeting. A nonentity. It's my job here.

"There's a problem," she says, looking at her stenographer's pad. This is not her office—it's a conference room after all—but she outranks the men. "But I have a new way."

This conference room must be at least forty stories in the air. There are billboard-sized windows converging across two walls, and the place is bright with midday sun and the sharp-edged veneer-fog that lit everything in the '80s. It is the '80s now. Her firm are like spies, or counter-terrorism brokers. They keep everything happening to make sure nothing happens. The rest of us are from all over, being here to do the job from our places where we do them best.

The problem, she will later realize (because I will later realize it, meaning I'm projecting or receiving things happening, but both to the same end) is that it is the '80s. What they've been doing can't be done in the '80s. People like us make sure time happens, too.

The men are listening, for certainly this fundamental problem is also the new problem.

"We can get a solid three minutes inside," she says, looking up. I retain more of her face this time when I look down and scratch her minutes onto my own stenographer's pad.

"We'll have to build this," she says, offering a diagram to the one with the voice we don't care about. He and Rashail and the third man are bothered by what they see. They know this is fundamentally impossible, 'getting inside' the way they've been doing. Building something to make it even more impossibly possible does not bode well for the anxieties they're already suffering. It makes everything they do a cry for help. An announcement of the problems they're having with simply being.

The edges and rooflines beyond the windows, though even more hazed than the objects in this room, do nothing ebulliently. Solidly. The outside is more stable than in.

"We'll lose lots of time just setting up and tearing down the equipment each night," Rashail says.

She agrees. This was also Penelope's plan, so now I have to wonder which of us is remembering Penelope. As if I didn't have plenty of other things worry about. I'm not very good at remembering people. Networking.

"There's a church we can use," third man says. "It's across the highway from my apartment—you can look down upon the entire property from my balcony."

I'm thinking '80s thoughts. Décor and the like, trying to decide what to expect in third man's place.

"He can keep watch," the one with the voice says. They all know he means me. I may have given them the idea with that line above. About deciding. We give each other ideas a lot. Everybody does.

I will have to attend several other meetings today, where I will take similar notes. This is my job.

A good story is supposed to contain three or more challenges, each situated after the other, each progressively more dangerous to either the character's or the reader's investment in the tale. This works because selves, discourse, religion, and cognition all work in the same manner. We look for ourselves in ourselves as often as we can, and wherever you find yourself, there you are. An open-ended search is not fun for anyone.

A good story is supposed to contain three or more challenges, and I have already either realized or created all three. This will not be a good story, but that is now your fault and not mine.

This is how I explain being in two places at once: networking. I'm standing upon third man's balcony, listening to the river of cars as they babble across the bridge below. There are city lights and nighttime everywhere. My binoculars are high-powered, so I've been watching the church property all night. No one has come or gone, so I have not used the walkie-talkie that is sitting on a small, dimpled-glass-topped balcony-table beside me. The walkie-talkie is as large as a shoebox and very heavy—third man bought it at an Army/Navy store.

I was dismayed to find his apartment decorated with lines and colors and furniture that was not possible in the '80s. It was similarly impossible in the '90s and in the '00s. Now I can't remember which of the decades I began this story with because how else would I know when these things ceased to be impossible?

The plan is going well inside the church, where I also am. Let me be clear, this is happening at the same time as I am keeping watch—at the same time as me listening to sampled, deconstructionist, college-rock that could be from any decade. It is being played by an unnecessary-to-identify device inside third man's apartment, which has just become necessary to identify. You could read this part of the story before you read the part about the balcony and the river and the night, and everything would be the same. It's not a problem that, if you're reading this part first, you don't know what I'm talking about, because you didn't read this part first.

Rashail is carrying the miter-saw into the van, where the one with the voice parked it earlier in the evening. Penelope is rolling and stapling the carpet back into place in a manner that indicates nothing has happened here during the night—that the church and its plumbing and its important wires will keep happening. The one with the voice has been collecting errant tools and wires for several minutes now. I'm not helping because I'm keeping watch, that's my job, I'm taking notes.

When everything is packed away, and I lower the binoculars for the last time, the sun has started to rise. Everyone leaves, and inside the church, it is clear that nothing has happened.

Sleep Walker

. . . Mammon led them on— / Mammon, the least erected Spirit that fell / From Heaven; for even in Heaven his looks and thoughts / Were always downward bent, admiring more . . . By him first / Men also, and by his suggestion taught, / Ransacked the centre, and with impious hands / Rifled the bowels of their mother Earth / For treasures better hid. . .

—John Milton, *Paradise Lost*, Book i, lines 678-88

HEN THE NOON BELLS GROANED, KENNETH LOOKED AT THE doors. Outside, stiff-backed pathfinders led the first wave of the post-church exodus. They ghosted stoically down the avenue, barely visible through the louvers. Next week, when the reverend mustered his militia outside, Kenneth would seal them more securely—he hated listening to the militia quote scripture.

To distract himself, he wiped down the bar—the drovers sitting across the room liked it. People expect a polishing barman, they'd told him. Though he valued their money, Kenneth wished they would just hand it all over now and be done with themselves. There'd been nothing performative about his ledgers in Boston, where he used to enjoy the Sunday clamor of different churches tolling different noons.

His rag skipped across the wood, hindered by the spirits in the varnish—the carpenter told him they would settle after a month or so. Kenneth didn't want them to—he didn't want anything to settle.

Bored, he watched the drovers stipple each other's shoes with sodden tobacco. Sunday might bring him only half a dozen throats, and he would hear Samuel's entire repertoire at least two dozen times. As rattled and uneven as the man played, he was the only one who had bought Kenneth's pitch on the place.

Outside, one of the parishioners abandoned the migration. Clutching a bowler against his chest, the fellow yielded the avenue with a bow to a trio of marching families. Suited in three pieces, the stranger looked more like a phantom from Kenneth's memory than one of the reverend's parch-throated farmers.

With his eyes on the man's paisley satchel, Kenneth wondered if he were in for another lecture about drinking.

The stranger shouldered his way inside the louvered doors and settled his bag on the bar. Kenneth could tell that—oiled, combed, and scented—the stranger was money. Northern money—not another farmer.

"Kenneth Lobert," the man requested, brushing at his sleeves.

Kenneth stopped polishing his bar. "Himself."

The stranger had eyes like cornflowers beneath the even rays of his blond hair. He extended his hand. "A pleasure."

Kenneth shook his hand—across the saloon, Samuel hammered out another terrible note. The drovers had traded their game for a good stare at the stranger's satchel.

The stranger opened it. "I'm Rigo St. James from Abrams and Company."

Kenneth brightened. "Oh, thank Christ—you got my letters."

"Right." Rigo extracted a ledger from his satchel, "Mr. Abrams is interested in you."

Kenneth sighed—he could save himself a match after all. "Well, a fair price—"

"Yes," Rigo leveled his gaze, "we don't want the saloon."

Kenneth hoped he'd misheard. To be so close . . .

When one of the drovers approached the bar, he retrieved a bottle by reflex.

"Now, one minute—" Kenneth started.

The drover leaned into their conversation. "More whiskey."

Kenneth obliged.

"See now," the drover addressed Rigo, "don't care much for 'baggers roundabouts."

Rigo settled a pince-nez on his aquiline nose. His smile looked forced, and it slid quickly down his narrow chin to disappear into his cravat.

"Yes, I see," Rigo said. "Perhaps I could offer a few drinks and leave you to your peace."

"That'd be about best."

"Wait—" Kenneth protested.

"One moment," Rigo said, fishing again through his satchel. He offered a silver dollar to the drover.

Kenneth relented when the drover tugged on the bottle. Nervous, he looked at Samuel—he'd stopped playing. With a wave, Kenneth started him up again.

The drover studied the coin. "This some 'bagger money?"

"Ask him." Rigo nodded at the other drover. "He'll know."

"Don't go nowhere."

"Certainly not."

Kenneth waited until the drover rejoined his companion.

"Mr. Abrams sent you," he said, "but he's not interested in my offer?"

Rigo studied his ledger. "Mr. Abrams is beginning territorial investments of his own—real estate, you see. I'm here to assure you that Abrams and Company will not threaten your business. If you're interested in cooperating . . ."

The drover started back for the bar.

". . . then I'll arrange the area."

What does that mean?

"This is some devil money!" the drover shouted, reaching for Rigo's shoulder.

"Currently, this is no town for a saloon," Rigo finished.

The drover spun him, dislodging the pince-nez. It clattered against Kenneth's planking and, in a dusty flash, caught an errant sunbeam. The lens bounced an oblong glint onto the drover's lapel.

"Did you hear me?" the drover shouted, balling his fists.

"Now wait—" Kenneth started. He could see the other drover inspecting Rigo's coin across the room. He hoped the man would calm his companion.

Rigo held the drover's gaze. "Are you interested in profit, Mr. Lobert?"

"Yes," Kenneth blurted, struggling to get his arms between the men. "Yes, of course."

"Then you'll cooperate."

The drover shook Rigo. "Answer me, damm you!"

"Yes!" Kenneth shouted. "Gentlemen, please!"

Rigo slapped a palm onto the bar. The stink of burning varnish curled between his fingers, and filigrees of smoke re-arranged the grain in the wood—for the briefest instant, Kenneth saw his own face in its squirming lines.

"Then we'll begin with murder," Rigo declared.

When the shot went off, Kenneth threw himself behind his bar. Shards of the great mirror behind the bar splashed every-where, and he could hear someone knocking down stools. He waited, but no one seemed to be moving.

He stood slowly.

Standing across the room, the other drover reloaded his gun. When Kenneth looked over the bar, he found the man's companion staining the floor with a chest wound.

Unperturbed, Rigo scribbled notes into his ledger. Kenneth stared at his bar. Rigo had somehow branded it with an . . . angled knot. Kenneth had never seen its like, and its alien curves dizzied him. Otherwise, the wood looked as normal as ever—his face, if it had ever actually been there, had disappeared from the grain.

"Tomorrow, then," Rigo said, hefting his satchel.

With effort, Kenneth summoned his voice. "Mr. St. James!"

Rigo turned.

Kenneth gestured at the brand. "What—"

"See that it's not disturbed," Rigo said, tipping his hat. Kenneth's doorway swallowed him in two door-swinging flashes of light.

The other drover slapped a coin onto the bar.

"I pay for my own drinks."

Kenneth nodded—the coin looked as ordinary as any other.

> *No one can serve two masters. He will either hate one and
> love the other, or be devoted to one and despise the other.
> You cannot serve God and mammon.*
> —Matthew 6:24

Kenneth's face itched, irritated by dust and sweat. Recalling the pock-marked statuary in the small park opposite his old firm in Boston, he imagined the dust scouring his skin into something marmoreal, something proper. The wind tugging his clothes snapped, searching, it seemed, for the New England parasols and coattails filling Kenneth's mind. He shoveled more gravel onto the corpse, and the resulting dust-clouds curled, disappearing with Kenneth's reverie upon the wind.

Reaching for more, Kenneth noticed the reverend and a pair of his militiamen. They had already crossed the avenue and were now snaking their way around the saloon.

He continued shoveling.

"Afternoon, Lobert."

Kenneth tossed more gravel. The winds grabbed at the newcomers' dusters, and the sun glinted in even dots along the men's ammunition belts. The varnished stocks of their guns looked almost wet inside their rawhide gussets.

"As is, Reverend," Kenneth said, resting a hand on his shovel.

The reverend's weak chin struggled with a smile. "It's good to see you at honest work."

Kenneth glanced at the grave.

"Well, 'idle hands . . .'" he intoned. Squinting against the sun, he hoped it looked like he was smiling.

The reverend folded his arms across his vest. Kenneth choked back a laugh when the man's monkeys followed suit.

"Have I given offense?" Kenneth asked. He could feel his palms getting muddy.

The reverend hefted another smile. "Not yet—just came with a word for your pile there."

Kenneth said nothing.

"So who is it, then?" the reverend asked, gesturing at the barrow.

With another glance at the trio's guns, Kenneth swallowed his sarcasm. He wondered if life would be any easier with a proper sheriff.

"Just a drover, sir."

"Shall I call a muster?"

"No," Kenneth said hurriedly. "T'were just a wage dispute."

He hated that they made him nervous. Their drawl seemed to steal so easily into his speech when they caught him off guard.

"As is," the revered countered, "I can't have a vigilante roundabouts."

"No, sir." Kenneth made sure they could see his smile now. "It's handled, sir."

The reverend fished a Bible from behind his lapel. "You agreed to control your guests."

Kenneth scratched his neck. "I will, sir—just a lapse is all. Honest drink's all I offer—no gunfighters."

Kenneth endured their silence.

"I've even got a sign," he added weakly.

"Move along now," the reverend said, removing his hat—the monkeys did likewise, "graveside's for believers."

"Yes, sir," Kenneth said, his footsteps awakening swirls of dust. It relieved him to re-enter the saloon. Sour as the purchase had been, the place was his. He'd have a drink before he helped Sam scrub the bloodstain.

Kenneth set the shovel under the bar and stared. Rigo's brand had softened. Most of the char had disappeared from the grooves, and the symbol had settled more smoothly into place. It looked less like a scar now—in fact, Kenneth thought it looked almost like some carver's sample: a single suggestion of what might be tiled in full across the walls.

The new brand beside it, though, bothered him even more than the first. He couldn't imagine its twisted loops and blackened angles on any wall, much less his.

How is he doing this?

Kenneth tossed an irritated glance at his patrons. The gunslinging drover had returned with a new companion. Kenneth disliked that the man hadn't at least selected a different table.

As a pair of newcomers found their way in, Kenneth covered the new brand with one of his rags. He hated that he looked such a mess to greet new arrivals—surveyors, he guessed by their packs.

As soon as he could, Kenneth made his way to the piano—Samuel had abandoned the bloodstain and was now plodding erratically through his repertoire.

"Did Mr. St. James come by?" Kenneth asked.

"Yessir," Samuel said, eyes on his keys. "Took some measurements—said he'd replace the mirror."

Kenneth glanced at it—the shards still clinging to the wall offered him strange, leaping images of his patrons. He had seen similar tableaux through stained-glass windows.

"Did he do anything to the bar?"

"Not that I saw, sir." Samuel tapped out his denouement and lifted a hand. Kenneth could see where the floor had tattooed Samuel's hands with the dead drover's blood. No doubt the chaotic dots would remain on Samuel's fingertips even after he'd dug the splinters out of them.

"I was at the stain all morning, sir."

"'Course you were, Sam."

When he heard footsteps, Kenneth turned. Rigo entered the saloon, a farmwife at his elbow and a satchel-laden youth behind. Dressed as dandily as Rigo, the boy was, no doubt, another 'bagger. Kenneth glanced at the drover, but the man had occupied himself with conversation.

"Mr. Lobert," Rigo called cheerily.

Kenneth waved and brushed self-consciously at his sleeves. While Rigo helped the farmwife to a table, the young 'bagger deposited his baggage beneath the window. He wasted no time extracting a ledger and taking notes.

Rigo approached the bar.

"Mr. St. James," Kenneth returned, eyeing the man's burgundy jacket, "I thought you'd be at real estate."

Rigo laughed.

"But I am. One is always at real estate."

Kenneth didn't feel like playing. He jerked the rag away from the new brand on his bar. "Tell me—what the hell is this?"

Rigo concealed the brand with his palm. "Mr. Lobert, that is not your concern."

"I didn't ask you to redecorate my bar."

Rigo lifted a manicured eyebrow. "Abrams and Company asks you to bear with us as we set things aright. There will be a few changes—"

"To a saloon you don't want?"

Rigo extracted a cigar from his pocket.

"You said you'd cooperate," he said, slipping the cigar between his lips. "My employers are interested in a flourishing saloon, even if they don't wish to own it. If you have changed your mind about our partnership, I can see to other arrangements."

Kenneth swallowed. He realized now that he'd never really shaken the heat of digging the drover's grave. When he lifted a hand to dab the sweat from his brow, he felt the muscles in his back convulse.

Rigo smiled mildly.

"No," Kenneth surrendered. "Your pardon—I'm overworked is all."

Rigo gestured, and the young 'bagger appeared, groomed, brushed, and wearing a blue crushed satin vest Kenneth envied. He wondered what had become of all the garments he'd left in Boston.

The youth smoothed his dark hair. Kenneth figured him for sixteen or so.

"I assumed you might need an extra tender," Rigo said, chewing on his cigar. "Lorenz works tirelessly—"

"But I can't—"

"And for free."

Kenneth poured whiskey. Even his elbows had begun to ache.

"Lorenz," Rigo said, sipping the drink, "see to the guests."

Rubbing his head, Kenneth didn't protest when Lorenz took the bottle and moved away.

"Now that woman," Rigo pointed, "is a new client. When she mentioned lodgings, I brought her immediately here."

Kenneth nodded. Sam's playing seemed worse than ever.

"If you like," Rigo said, "I'll negotiate on your behalf." "Of course," Kenneth said, withdrawing another bottle.

"You won't restrict her comings and goings—nor the arrival of her callers?"

"She's free to do as she likes," Kenneth downed his drink, "as long as she can pay."

"Of course," Rigo said, plucking the cigar from his mouth. "She's just after a bit of freedom, is all—hard time at home, you see."

Kenneth looked at her. She looked no different than any of the other women who normally strolled the avenue. "Hasn't she got a place?"

Rigo stared. "Well, now—she's interested in yours, Kenneth. Shall I turn her away?"

No.

Rigo gestured again, and Lorenz faced him immediately. After the briefest pause, the boy crossed the room and settled a whiskey glass before the farmwife.

"I'll just see to the details," Rigo said, striking a match.

When, without warning, Kenneth's knees buckled, he slammed his palms onto the bar. It didn't matter that the drover was leaving, even if the man had become his longest-standing regular. Kenneth just wanted to lie down.

Lorenz appeared behind the bar and slid Kenneth's arm across his shoulders. Without a word, he started for the stairs.

"My bar . . ." Kenneth said, suddenly nauseated.

"Sam and I will see to it," Rigo said.

Kenneth thought he saw the bar smoking again, but struggling as he was toward the stairs, he couldn't be sure.

"Mr. Lobert?" Samuel asked, rising.

"Listen to Mr. Saint James, Sam. I've got to lie down."

Samuel frowned. "As you like, sir."

*. . . and [even] among the invisible beings there were
some that had [been constrained] to labour for him by his
Sustainer's leave—and whichever of them deviated from
Our command, him would We let taste suffering through
a blazing flame; they made for him whatever he wished of
sanctuaries, and statues . . .*
    —The Qu'ran, Surah 34:12

Drifting through fever dreams, Kenneth listened to a new song. He'd heard of composers in Europe using strange noises and arrhythmic percussion to shock their audiences. One had even started a riot.

Buried in the noise, a sonata laughed through its scales, dipping flirtatiously into heartbeat chords. Kenneth picked a hammer from the accompanying tumult, a dumb lament slapping after the melody. He heard laughter, a saw, the chiming of busy drinks. Once or twice, the basso thud of steamer trunks resounded on the stairs. He smiled. Certainly the music would never fill any New England hall, but if this was the best he'd find on the frontier, so be it.

When the harping of a snake-oil mountebank shrieked an aria into the suite, Kenneth sighed—the man had the same voice as the speculator who'd sold him the saloon.

Shuddering awake, he squirmed out of his damp bed. Someone had left him a pitcher and a bottle, so he took a swig from each. Spending a moment with the chamber pot, he noticed that it had been emptied. He had only barely relieved himself when the backs of his eyes made a grab at his brain. He blinked rapidly, hoping to clear the starbursts blooding his vision. The pain eased, and after a moment, he registered the moonlight falling across the infinite grid of a columned atrium.

What the hell?

Kenneth sat, spellbound, vision captured by the strange symbols adorning the room. Mosaics crawled seamlessly across curving joists and balustrades—though he knew, somehow, that such architectural names meant nothing here: they hadn't been created yet.

He must be delirious. This was not his room over the saloon.

Men in loincloths drained the water from hoppers pregnant with olive oil. Women, festooned with dangling tin, approached with trays. Dazed, he smoothed his hand across a divan, his gaze trapped by the gaping halves of the women's scant blouses. Their breasts hung suspended in the moonlight, shut out by the incapable garments, glowing. With a start, he dropped his gaze onto his own breasts. They curved into his noblewoman's vestments, a celebration of his mercantile power. His hips ached a bit where they swelled upon the couch.

A blonde woman approached with the first draw from the hoppers. Kenneth knew they were his wealth. He'd negotiated their exportation with another woman just this morning. By next week, his atrium would veritably thrum with new trade—already he'd received word from more than a dozen other Minoans who wished to rent chambers for the event.

"Was it worth the wait?" the blonde asked, extending her ewer with a bow. The blonde's handmaidens stood blankly behind her, dark, their chests concealed in servitude.

Kenneth smiled. "Of course."

He tossed a soft glance at one of the mosaics, and his hips ossified back into themselves—narrow again, masculine.

It surprised him to become aware once more of the weight of his penis. His chambers in the saloon had restored him, it seemed. Even now, he remembered only blue tile and a woman with oil.

It took him long moments to negotiate his tangled thoughts and cross the room. He noticed that the piano had fallen from the suite that accompanied his fever. The rest of the cacophony remained.

Clumsily, he unlatched the window. The wind brought him a frisson of chilly vertigo. Kenneth grabbed the sill and looked at the avenue. The faithful had installed a few new lamps, and there was more traffic than normal. A moment later, he spotted the mountebank who'd pierced his fever. Kenneth had certainly never seen him before.

It took him long minutes to realize that quivering guy-lines now cordoned almost an entire new block across from his saloon. Stakes and lanterns and lumber lay everywhere, surveyors and carpenters like busy insects amidst. Across the road, a team of oxen marched, snorting. The frame of something massive, something vaulted, climbed rigidly behind them.

He became belatedly aware of a tumult below. His saloon sounded packed, and he could hear someone sawing on the blind side of his back wall. He didn't care if it disturbed the drover's grave out there.

At length, he noticed Rigo along one of the cordons. The man held his bowler in one hand, gesturing at a nearby companion. Kenneth watched them shake hands. When the stranger walked away, rubbing his palm, Kenneth recognized him: Samuel.

Why isn't he at the piano?

Sam moved away, and Kenneth wondered if his fever was rallying, for the sonata returned a few moments later.

But Sam can't . . .

Kenneth watched, alarmed, as riders fogged the edges of the block with upflung dust. Rigo, it appeared, took the same notice. He strode evenly into the avenue, adjusting his bowler with delicate fingers. Kenneth couldn't tell if the riders were marauders or militia. By their gunshots, though, they had come armed. A flash of movement below caught his eye. He hadn't noticed that a coach had hitched itself beneath his overhang. Shadowed arms slammed its doors shut.

A stage? Now?

He looked again at Rigo. Staring down the advancing riders, Rigo lifted a halting palm. When the reverend's militia started advancing from the other direction, reciting Scripture in a polyrhythmic gibber, Rigo pivoted. He lifted his other arm in a similar gesture, standing rigid and well-dressed like a new road sign. Kenneth thought he looked like Jesus, standing there with his arms spread.

Without warning, the air congealed, filling the lane with a carrion stench. Kenneth's stomach heaved, and blessedly, he collapsed onto the floor. Lights like flashpowder tongued his windowsill, and the militia harmonized its scripture with what sounded like an entire town's worth of impassioned glossolalia. Shots went off, things sizzled, and his fever slipped its dark arms back around his brain.

Samuel played magnificently.
Somehow, he played magnificently.

———

The mind is its own place, and in itself / Can make a Heav'n of Hell, a Hell of Heav'n," / says Satan. He later realizes: / "Which way I flie is Hell; my self am Hell."
—John Milton, *Paradise Lost*

Leaning over the well in the center of his broch, Kenneth could see the tide coming. His freshwater trembled, shaken now and then by the ocean's long-standing quarrel with the cliffs. Soon, he would smell the rising waters through the windows his wife had demanded for the back wall. Looking, he admired her dusk-limned silhouette more than the view of the ocean. She stood, humming songs for her dead brothers, staring at the waves. Her loosened hair shone along its tips, quenched, in places, by the dipping knots still tucked in her great braid. The broch's rounded walls cupped the dusklight with stone fingers. Kenneth loved that they tossed the gloaming at his wife's back—she'd helped him survey the land when the architect offered to build.

With a cough, the architect emerged from the stairs between the walls. He'd had the grace to don Kenneth's tartan, though Kenneth knew that would change as soon as the man found another lord. Brochs were rising like boils everywhere the Scoti could place them.

"Have you seen to the field lords?" Kenneth asked. He'd only recently negotiated their lease on his southern pasture. Removing the old tenants had been bloody, but the survivors loved the new hall down the hill. Already, travelers had started appearing for a night's stay, some meager trade, and a few black-jacks of grain ale.

The architect offered a pale smile. "Indeed, lord—the tenants are pleased."

Kenneth disliked the Roman stain on the man's voice.

"And they've brought their . . . 'iron'?" he asked.

The architect dragged a finger across the wall, tracing and tracing his odd mason's symbol. Kenneth had indulged him the mark only because he had worked so quickly.

The architect glanced at Kenneth's sun-reddened wife. "Two hundred swords by winter."

"Good," Kenneth grunted, looking once more at his wife. He hoped for another son by spring.

"Get your darkling to work, then," Kenneth ordered. The architect's apprentice bothered him, stealing about so silently, so darkly, as he did.

Kenneth gestured at his wife. "And she'll make no deal with you, not tonight, so be about your scribbling and leave us."

The architect left, and Kenneth abandoned the well. As he stepped into place beside his wife, she eased the cloak she'd been clutching around his shoulders. When, strangely, the earth heaved, he extended an arm to check his fall. The broch seemed suddenly filled with a thousand unwanted guests. They made a dark cloud of his thoughts. Confused, he tried to understand where his wife had gotten her now-black garments. The fever wasn't gone—in fact, it seemed worse. His skin tightened in expanding rings, the dead lapping of an evaporating dream.

His wife, in New England formalwear, stretched and leaned, negotiating Kenneth's uncooperative arms through a jacket. She had already secured a cravat around his neck. Kenneth studied her. Draped and tucked with dark lace, she looked like some spectral debutante. Her skin gleamed, pale, along her neck and into her gown, reminding Kenneth suddenly of the saloon-girls he'd been promised when he bought the place.

He'd hoped they would sit in the windows at sunset.

What are these dreams?

"Back among the living, Mr. Lobert?"

Kenneth looked. Rigo lounged in a salon chair, smoking as he studied a pocketwatch.

Kenneth settled his jacket with a shrug. Something shivered again, deep beneath the saloon, and the tails of his jacket brushed the backs of his legs.

"What's all this?" Kenneth asked.

"Well, this," Rigo gestured at the woman, "Is Vanesse— she'll be your lady this evening."

Kenneth studied her. She lowered her eyes, and he could see his lamplight reflected on the cosmetic rouging her eyelids. She looked familiar.

"Why so much black?" he ventured, feeling again as though it weren't just the three of them in his chamber.

"Mourning, sir," she said. "My good husband crossed one of our drovers this moon past—to his death."

He recognized her—a wife.

Someone's farmwife.

"Murdered?" Kenneth asked, thinking vaguely of heathered fields and grass-bearded hillocks.

"As was," she conceded. It bothered Kenneth that she smiled. For the briefest instant, he noticed something within her. Something squirmed, adjusted, and re-settled beyond his notice.

Did he hear it humming?

He lost his balance as the unhappy whatever thrashed again belowground. Neither Vanesse nor Rigo seemed to notice.

"What the hell is going on?" Kenneth demanded. "Is there a quake?"

Rigo tucked his watch away. "There's no quake, Mr. Lobert— some tenants create greater disturbances than others. Don't worry, it's not bothering anyone else."

Rigo smiled. "Abrams and Company has added two new wings to your saloon—neither has found even a disturbed eyelash for your newest guest."

"You've added on?"

"Many things have changed," Rigo said. "You're now the richest man this side of Mason's Line."

Kenneth glanced around his chambers. They weren't the same. He now had astral lamps, leathern furniture, proper wallpaper— he could even see what looked like a study through a small hallway and a pair of doors.

The sensation of crowds re-filled the chamber, and swarms upon swarms of displeased somethings made a churning froth of Rigo's cornflower eyes. He shied from the sight of it. He looked instead at Vanesse, and already he wasn't sure he'd seen anything at all.

Rigo pressed a finger against his forehead and sighed. "Some clients—it unnerves them to wait."

Vanesse appeared at Kenneth's side, a top-hat between her fingers. He accepted it reflexively.

"Your newest guest," Rigo said, "requires a great deal of accommodation."

Kenneth felt suddenly as if he were floating, as if the entire saloon had taken to some current on an inland sea.

"Is he . . . blasting?" Kenneth ventured, securing his hat. "Has he got dynamite?"

Rigo laughed. "Oh, no."

Vanesse giggled as she slipped her fingers around Kenneth's elbow.

"The new arrival is a woman, a most well-bred and highborn woman, Mr. Lobert. And the earth heaves to greet her because she is pooling its dark blood outside of town."

"Blood? Do you mean . . . oil?" Kenneth asked.

"Oh, yes." Rigo's eyes sparkled. "No one knows it's there yet, but they will—oh, how they will. Don't worry—she and I have already drawn up contracts in your name.

"Her sister—lovely woman—is summoning gold to the hills."

"I suppose I have contracts there as well?" Kenneth asked unsteadily.

"Of course."

Kenneth closed his eyes. "What you're describing is not possible."

It's a dream.

Rigo tsked. "Your Bostonian philosophers like to think that the world they see is a great, dumb wasteland—an inanimate heap upon which they may run about and be brilliant."

Vanesse pressed herself against Kenneth. This could be no dream. Glancing at her, he realized now that the tissue around her eyes looked unhealthily reddened. His spine ached.

"But reality," Rigo continued, eyes shivering as the host re-awakened behind them, "is a mélange of interested parties, and man, I'm afraid, is the smallest broker at the table."

He cinched his bowler into place. At his gesture, Vanesse opened the chamber door.

"But, weak as he may be," Rigo said, handing Kenneth a lacquered cane, "man holds all the real estate."

Rigo gestured him forward, and Kenneth approached the door. He became aware of the something within Vanesse thrumming excitedly. Her chest heaved as her fingers slipped from his elbow to his hand, and he fought the urge to recoil.

"Does something inhabit you?" he asked, greeted in the hallway by an immaculate piano suite.

"Why, Mr. Lobert," she said, producing a fan in her off hand, "now that you're recovered, I'm hoping you will. What, with last night going so pleasantly and all."

Rigo prodded them. "Hurry now, the others are waiting. You've proven so difficult to make ill, Mr. Lobert, I'd hate to spoil your poor health."

"What?" Kenneth asked, moving with Vanesse. "But—I've been ill."

"Oh," Rigo shook his head, "you've been anything but. I think I may have found smallpox for you this time. You should have several good weeks to enjoy the fruits of your cooperation with Abrams and Company."

Kenneth felt like an idiot child, like an imposter at his parents' table. When he glanced at Vanesee, he could see that a film of sweat now lined her brow. He decided that she must be ill as well.

Rigo checked his watch again. "We must see what we can while we can, though. Your guests will re-establish your health soon enough."

He looked at Kenneth. "And you'll sleep again in your perfect, useful health."

"My guests?" Kenneth asked. He realized he must sound simple speaking almost entirely in questions. "Are there surgeons in the new wings?"

"It's all spelled out on your bar," Rigo said. "You'll notice that others' contracts now adorn the walls and ceiling— it looks nice."

"I need some whiskey," Kenneth said.

The last of the well-wishers to leave his porch shook Kenneth's hand. Rigo stood nearby, tapping his cane, and Vanesse had tightened her grip on Kenneth's arm to keep from being dislodged by the crowd. He was still reeling from seeing so many people in the saloon. Rigo had only barely been able to shoulder a path though the mob, so Kenneth hadn't had time to penetrate the cluster around the piano, where Sam played beautifully. Lorenz worked in a dark blur behind the bar. Kenneth saw the youth stash several coins in the till in the span of only a few seconds. Rigo had replaced the mirror with a stained-glass mosaic.

Dazed, Kenneth now watched groups of pedestrians stroll the avenue. Buildings had gone up everywhere. The great edifice he'd noticed during his delirium had become a small concert hall. Well-dressed patrons had filed themselves neatly before its doors. A banner hung from its barge-boards, heralding a premiere.

As in his chambers, Kenneth felt as if there were a great many more people in town than he could see. Most of the pedestrians hosted one of Rigo's somethings. Unlike Vanesse and himself, these others didn't appear content to nest quietly behind their hosts' eyes. They were in control, and despite the activity around him, Kenneth felt as if he were standing in a crowd of sleepwalkers.

"You see now that you've made some new friends," Rigo said.

Kenneth eyed him. "I don't remember any of this."

"Come along."

Kenneth followed unhappily. When a horseman interrupted their path, Kenneth studied him. The drover who'd murdered his companion regarded Kenneth emptily. Lamplight glinted on the sheriff's badge pinned to the man's lapel.

With a tip of his hat, the drover moved on.

Kenneth turned to Vanesse.

"Sorry, gentlemen," she said, addressing a cluster of pleading workmen, "I'm not entertaining this evening. Bring your coins to the saloon tomorrow—it'll be business as usual."

The solicitors, Kenneth noticed, looked more than simply crestfallen—they looked terrified. These, inhabited like everyone else, were not sleepwalking. They looked just as awake as Vanesse, and Kenneth could almost smell the disease upon them. They resembled waxen effigies when the moonlight slicked the undersides of their chins with rainwater reflections.

Wait, rainwater?

Their pleas bounced off of moistened cobbles, and Kenneth found himself hoping that the guards patrolling nearby would move along. He hated how their crimson tabards cast bloody glimmers on their polished halberds. Their queen's manse sulked on the hill in the distance, tolling its dictatorial bells. Kenneth hoped there weren't messages coded into the chimes. If the guards were going to come for him, they should do so by honest means.

Studying Vanesse's houppelande, Kenneth knew they had to vacate the lane before the priests' march filed into the whores' quarter. Nervously, he tugged on his hose as he searched for a convenient escape between all the thatch-and-plaster apartments. The rest of his whores, ambulating like cottony moths around him, would have to see for themselves. He was only taking Vanesse with him. He couldn't afford another week in the sinner's stocks. Not now.

Where was . . .

Ahead, back on the dirt lane, Rigo had begun conversing with a passing couple. Kenneth forced himself to tip his hat when the bonneted woman smiled.

Things are slipping.

He turned to Vanesse. "Are you a prostitute?"

She cut a glance at him. "Lady of the evening."

I've gone mad.

Kenneth thought of her first visit to his saloon. "'Callers'?"

She studied him. "I needed freedom."

"Rigo murdered your husband," Kenneth realized aloud, wondering if any of this had actually happened. Tiles and spearheads and seaside walls effervesced through his attention. He couldn't tell which was his past and which the fever's.

She looked away. "My father brokered that marriage. I didn't mind undoing it. Besides," she added, "Rigo didn't kill him. The sheriff did."

Other pedestrians gathered around Rigo, so Kenneth pulled Vanesse further away.

"What has been going on here?" he asked. "Am I hallucinating? How could the reverend let the sheriff get away with murder? Why does this place keep changing?"

She didn't resist, so Kenneth kept moving. People in togas flashed like shades through his periphery.

"Part of a sheriff's duty is to enforce contracts, wouldn't you say?" she asked, waving away clients with skin like copper. Kenneth knew he'd seen their headdresses somewhere before.

No I haven't, he assured himself. I haven't seen any of this!

Kenneth thought about the seals on his bar. "You mean the sheriff sees to Rigo's deals."

Vanesse shrugged. "As you like."

He turned onto an avenue he'd never seen. Sandstone blocks lined the road in pyramidal walls.

"We all made agreements with Mr. St. James," she said. "Look around."

It's the fever.

Kenneth didn't have to look. He could feel unnatural crowds swelling everywhere. "Yes, but in exchange for what?"

He noticed a few of the reverend's militiamen ushering people along the avenue—the actual avenue. Tugging on Vanesse, he marched after them. Certainly, despite everything else, he should be able to rouse the reverend. Kenneth couldn't imagine how the man had countenanced such deviltry in the town.

That is, Kenneth thought, if something hasn't already happened to him.

"Rigo came and arranged things," Vanesse said, "he put them aright."

"Things are changing," Kenneth said dumbly, watching campaniles faze through the moonlight like cheap paintings. He recalled an evening beneath them, a deal with men in cloaks. The Freemasons didn't like what he was doing in White Chapel.

The church bells chimed the hour. Colonial facades and side-streets now stood where the church once had. When Kenneth glanced behind him, ambling crowds filled his wake. He didn't see Rigo anywhere.

"And why don't I remember any of the process?" he said. Someone brushed his elbow, muttering in guttural Latin.

"Because you're full of desire," Vanesse hissed, struggling to keep pace. "Everyone is. Don't you see? It's given you Boston out here. It's given you what you wanted."

"This is not Boston."

Kenneth looked at her, watching as she folded her hands across her abdomen.

"I wanted freedom," she admitted, "so Mr. St. James filled me with it, but not all desire is as dumbing as yours, Kenneth."

She met his gaze. "Only illness brings you back to yourself."

The fever.

"And where is the reverend in all this?"

She started them walking again. "In his church, converting all these surveyors and prospectors, training gunmen for the borders. He plays host to his own desires."

Kenneth spotted a cluster of masons hammering at a block of marble. It looked as if they were sculpting a fountain.

"It's not supposed to work this way," he said. "This isn't natural."

The crowd had noticed Kenneth. He still couldn't see Rigo, but people everywhere were muttering about the premiere. Kenneth couldn't be late for the premiere. It wouldn't be proper.

He glared at the gathering throng. Between the shoulders of the congealing mass, he saw the slender flèche climbing the new church. It shifted, assembling shingles and donning paint before Kenneth's eyes. Clusters of tents flapped and swelled alongside the sanctuary below, and hymns droned upon the wind. The church had attracted crowds of its own. It looked to Kenneth as if there were a revival going on.

Searching for a way out, Kenneth issued Vanesse behind him.

"And how is it you know so much?" he asked.

In only a few nauseating maneuvers, the mob scabbed itself around them. Kenneth batted at the multi-colored arms pawing at them. Somewhere, a scimitar flashed.

"We need you at the premiere," he heard.

Someone snarled. "You're not in your place, Mr. Lobert."

Kenneth seized Vanesse's wrist and started throwing elbows. After only a few tries, he started connecting. The blows felt as if he were wedging rail-spikes into his arm.

He felt awake. Relieved, he noticed that the architecture had stopped changing around him. Everyone appeared temporally appropriate.

I must be getting better.

Dragging Vanesse, Kenneth renewed his flight.

But Rigo promised me weeks. Whose worlds are these?

A number of the mob had all taken up the same chant. "We all have our place, Mr. Lobert."

"Where are we going?" Vanesse asked.

Kenneth charged toward the church.

Inside the sanctuary, he found even more people. They ambled between pews, shaking hands, praying. Some had already started singing. A few noticed Kenneth and waved. He waved back, his attention on their guns. Hurriedly, he scanned the unfamiliar sanctuary.

Vanesse clutched his arm more tightly. "You're not the stranger here you think you are."

Settling on a doorway, Kenneth threaded toward it. "You're telling me I'm a believer now?"

"Of course you are," she said. "You're the town's greatest philanthropist. Where else would you spend your Sundays?"

How else do I spend my time?

He opened the first door he came to and jerked Vanesse inside. Even the faithful had begun murmuring about the premiere. In the semi-darkness of what now looked like a classroom, he took Vanesse by the shoulders.

"We have smallpox, right?"

"It's going around."

"You stay sick all the time?" he prompted. "This is your 'freedom'? This is how you stay awake?"

"In one way or another," she said. "My callers are a sick lot."

"We need an exorcist," he said, approaching a shadowed desk. "I need an exorcist."

"It wouldn't work."

"Why not?"

"Where do you think Rigo found his clients in the first place? He is an exorcist. He keeps quarters here, in the church.

Kenneth rifled through a drawer. "Don't be ridiculous. This is all becoming just god-damned ridiculous."

He found a pistol. When he yanked it free, bullets scattered in wobbling circles beneath. He grabbed them.

Vanesse stomped across the room. The faithful had begun clapping and chanting outside.

"Listen, Kenneth," she said. "Rigo collects desire. It's been to Greece, it found London, he brought it to Boston, and now it's here—collected and deposited safely away from everything else."

Kenneth stood, gun in one hand, bullets in the other. "You're saying we're some sort of quarantine?"

"Reverend calls them demons," she said. She tapped his brow with a thin finger. "They have to live somewhere. People don't want them in civilized places."

Real estate.

"And eventually?"

Tenants.

"When the town's in order, he re-collects and finds some place to start again. He's mentioned California."

"And in the meantime?" Kenneth pressed.

She gestured to the room, twirling. "Business as usual."

But what stays behind?

Kenneth felt a smile. He hoped it was his and not his tenant's. As the revival thundered into full momentum, he stepped around the desk and set down his gun. He brushed at Vanesse's waxen face. "You can wake everybody. You can make them all ill."

She looked at the floor. "I do what I can."

Kenneth opened his palm. The weak light curled around the sleeping bullets. "If you could just give these a kiss"

Time to get up.

She settled her eyes on the bullets. "You don't mean to—"

"Oh, I mean to," he promised, adjusting his hat. "Won't kill no one, now will it? Certainly demons can survive gunshots."

She finally smiled.

Kenneth turned to the door as she lifted the first bullet to her lips.

"Where are you going?" she asked.

"Am I contagious?" he asked.

"Of course, but—"

He put his hand on the latch. "Give me a minute with the baptistery. We'll take our bullets downtown right after."

Song like thunder replaced the door when he opened it. All the stomping set the walls to vibrating. It felt as if Kenneth's quake-guest had got to work here as well. Behind him, something roared through the clash of cheap swords.

He cupped a hand to his mouth. "Don't worry," he shouted, barely audible over the coliseum's noise, "we'll make the premiere."

Vanesse kissed another bullet.

"After all," he called, "we're expected."

end

Publication Notes

- "Light Both Foreign and Domestic" (previously unpublished)
- "Hotels and Other Forms of Collapse" (*3:AM Magazine*–November, 2007)
- "Two" (*Hatter Bones*–2009)
- "The Basement, Borges" (*Diet Soap*–November, 2007)
- "Slipstring" (*Sein und Werden*–2008)
- "'Seng, Running" (*PostScripts*–December, 2009)
- "Fairyland" (*Coffinmouth*–September, 2011)
- "They Would Only be Roads" (*Paper Cities: An Anthology of Urban Fantasy*–2008; audio, *District of Wonders*, 2015)
- "The Dust and the Red" (*Apex Magazine*–March, 2011)
- "∞°" (*Electric Velocipede*–Fall, 2010)
- "The Heresy Box" (*Polyphony #6*–2006)
- "Sweet Water" (previously unpublished)
- "Syntagm" (*Moon Milk Review*–Fall, 2011)
- "Stormchasing" (previously unpublished)
- "How Nothing Happens" (*Cyber World: Tales of Humanity's Tomorrow*)
- "Sleepwalker" (*Needles & Bones*)

About the Author

Darin is the bestselling author of *Noise*, *Chimpanzee*, and *Totem*. He was the founding fiction editor of the experimental ezine *Farrago's Wainscot*, and he has taught courses on writing and literature at several universities. He now works as an editor in media journalism. He lives in Texas with his wife.

www.darinbradley.com